"I have a confession to make. I am hopelessly and irredeemably in love with the short story. I can't get enough of them. And so, when I was asked to take a sneak peek at Gruesome Faces, Ghastly Places, a collection of stories from Doug Murano, C.W. LaSart and Adrian Ludens, I jumped at the chance, and I'm so glad that I did. I knew I would like this book, but I wasn't expecting to put it away in one sitting. These three voices, brought together here like a chorus, are part of the cutting edge of modern horror. Go ahead and turn the page. I dare you. But I will warn you. You're gonna get sliced up. And you'll love it while you bleed. They're that good."
-Joe McKinney, Bram Stoker Award® winning author of *Plague of the Undead* and *Dead World Resurrection*

"LaSart, Ludens, and Murano prove power trios aren't only for rock and roll. Like great rock music, the stories in Gruesome Faces, Ghastly Places will send a chill down your spine and leave you wanting more."
-James Chambers, author of *The Engines of Sacrifice* and *Three Chords of Chaos*

"When a collaboration of talented horror writers such as these, join forces in a collection of dark tales such as this, the only outcome is sure to keep you reading with the lights on!"
-Rena Mason, Bram Stoker Award® winning author of *The Evolutionist* and *East End Girls*

"The official State motto of South Dakota is 'Under God, the people rule.' After reading the stories in Gruesome Faces, Ghastly Places, you might decide that a less beneficent entity or two is in charge and that the people seldom rule and often barely survive. In the very best way, this collection reminds me of the classic 'Hitchcock Presents' paperbacks: The horror here initially seems familiar and then takes twists and turns, zigs, zags, and deadfalls into new and ultra-disturbing places. South Dakota will not likely add this title as a guidebook, but if you like traveling with fear as a companion, you'll want this collection of G and G."

-Mort Castle, Bram Stoker Award® winning author of *New Moon on the Water* and Bram Stoker Award® winning contributing editor (with Sam Weller) to *Shadow Show: Stories in Celebration of Ray Bradbury*

# Gruesome Faces, Ghastly Places

# DOUG MURANO
# C.W. LASART
# ADRIAN LUDENS

Cover and interior illustrations: Luke Spooner, www.carrionhouse.com

Copyright © 2014 Slanted Mansion Books
All rights reserved.
ISBN: 0692302956
ISBN-13: 978-0692302958

# ACKNOWLEDGMENTS

The authors wish to extend special thanks to Joe McKinney, Rena Mason, James Chambers, and Mort Castle for graciously taking time out of their busy schedules to read our collection and share their thoughts.

Adrian thanks: My wife Crissy, and our kids, Victor and Maddy. Everyone who has ever critiqued my stories and helped me learn from my mistakes. Thanks also to the editors who have purchased my stories and to Doug and C.W. for being fantastic to work with. Thank you to everyone who reads for pleasure.

Doug thanks: My wife, Jessica, for giving me time. Rocco, Eva, and little bean, for giving me courage. My readers, for giving me a reason. My mother and father, for setting me upon good paths. My mentors, for lighting the way. Special thanks, also, to my two collaborators. I'm glad we're friends.

C.W. thanks: For every story written, there are many people in the background that make it possible. I would like to thank my family for putting up with me when I am in a "writing" mood, my personal editor, Kacy Danek, without whom, my voice would be lost, and last but not least, Adrian Ludens and Doug Murano, my partners in crime and fellow South Dakota horror writers!

# CONTENTS

**C.W. LASART:**

# THE CHOPPING BLOCK

## *Doug Murano*

I remember the chopping block.

Papa raised the hatchet up above his head and over Lucy's neck. I didn't want to watch this part, but Papa said I need to see how it was done. One day, he said, I would have to do this by myself. Papa reminded me that Lucy would only hurt for a moment and that she might run around before she forgot everything bad that's ever happened to her and go to sleep.

"Remember, we have to take a life to give it to ourselves, sweetheart," he said. It's what he always said. "You can't think twice about it."

Lucy lay still between Papa's big hand and the big oak stump. She looked at all the red dents in the wood where the hatchet had cut before. Her head was right down by all little fluffy feathers stuck in the oak, but she didn't wiggle around or try to get away because Papa handled all the chickens right out of the shell. That way, they learned to trust him and they stayed quiet and gentle when we came into the chicken coop to take their eggs in the morning. And they never struggled at the block.

Sometimes, we left the eggs right where they were in the nests and let the hens sit on them so they hatched to become little chickens that might lay eggs someday, too. Sometimes, one of the little chickens hatched with too many wings, crooked feet or eyes so big and purple they looked like big blind blueberries. When that happened, Papa took them away and used an old rusty spade to bury them behind the house. Papa said that's the way things are in the world now. We never, ever ate the sick ones.

Sometimes, we took one of the hens to the chopping block, and then we had chicken for supper. We never took Ricky to the block because he helped the hens get their eggs. Ricky got cranky when we came into the chicken coop and he kicked his heels at Papa's legs. We used to have another rooster Papa named Ricardo but Ricky pecked his eyes out, and it was out to the block and into the pot with Ricardo, so after that we only ever had one boy at a time.

I liked how the chicken smelled when Papa cooked it over the fire or in an old pot on the old iron stove in the farmhouse. It tasted like heaven, but I cried every time we visited the block. Papa said it was important to give them names even if we ate them, because in this world it's important to learn how to say goodbye to everything we love, like when we said goodbye to Mama after the lights and fires started. I can still hear her voice in my head if I close my eyes, telling me to be not to be afraid, but I can't see her face anymore.

Papa asked me if I was ready, and I said I was. He said, "Don't look away now. Don't you close your eyes." He stretched his arm up high, and Lucy closed her eyes but I didn't. I looked right at her and waited for Papa to come down on her with the hatchet.

I remember the day the men came.

Papa and me were getting eggs from the nests in the chicken coop. None of the hens were upset that we were stealing their eggs. They didn't make a sound. Papa held Marilyn up so he could reach underneath her, then Papa's shoulders jumped a little like a bee stung him, and he turned his face to the doorway and looked off into the distance behind my shoulder.

"Papa?" I asked.

"Shh!" said Papa, and he handed Marilyn to me. She clucked. "Listen."

I did, and I could hear the wind shooshing through the tall grass around the farmyard. I turned around to look out of the door and I could see forever. Papa said that all that space kept us safe. I heard a thump-thump-thump-thump and my eyes followed the sound to a puff of dirt way far away. When I squinted up my eyes, I could see two little dots bouncing around in the dust way across the river. They were the first visitors we'd had since we left the city.

"You get inside," said Papa, and took the hatchet down off the wall and handed that to me too. "Get down under the floor like we practiced and don't come back out until you know for sure you're alone or until I come and get you. And if anyone finds you that isn't me, you bury this part right between his eyes."

I ran through the weed patch, past the chicken coop and through the doorway into the house, holding the hatchet in one hand and Marilyn under my other arm like she was my baby. The wood floor was old and gray and cracked. It was cool on my feet.

I used to fit better because I was smaller before, and the last time I practiced, I had to curl up tight. This time when Marilyn and I got down there, it felt like the cold dirt and the roots would close in on my shoulders and swallow me up whole.

Marilyn tucked her head underneath her wing and went to sleep. She didn't understand anything or maybe she didn't care. I wished I could be like her.

Papa's footsteps thumped across the floorboards inside the house. I heard shuffling and metal sounds as he grabbed his pistol and bullets. Then I heard clack-clackity of his bullets bouncing off the floor.

"Fuck-all!" Papa said.

The thump-thump-thump of horses' hooves was close now.

"Who's in that house?" said a man from outside.

"Just an old man and his hens," I heard Papa say. "You're welcome to one or two if you'd like."

Then those men just started shooting for no good reason at all.

I remember when we first came to the house.

It felt like we had walked forever, but Papa said we had to get far away from the cities and all the people left there. He said folks weren't like they used to be and probably never would be again.

I saw the farmhouse up on the hilltop before Papa did. "Oh Papa, it's perfect! Is this far enough?"

"I don't know. Wait here," said Papa and he fished his pistol out of the old bag he carried. He opened the gun and eyed down the chamber to make sure it was loaded and started off. "Get down in the grass and I'll come find you again when I've looked around."

I watched him walk across the open field until the dark open doorway swallowed him up. He was gone a long time, and I stayed down just like he told me. Then I heard the swish-swish of Papa walking through the grass. He smiled like I hadn't seen in a long time.

"I have a surprise for you," he said and led me up to the house.

When we got to the house, Papa took me around back and showed me the chickens pecking around the farmyard.

"They're beautiful, Papa," I said. "Why did they stay here with nobody to take care of them?"

"I guess they know where home is," said Papa.

"Is it home for us? Can we stay here forever?" I asked.

"I don't know about forever, but I think this might be a good place to be right now. Mama would approve."

We stayed there and felt happy. The weather got warm and the days got long. Papa gave the chickens names and taught them to me. Lucy. Marilyn. Ethel. Ricky. Papa and I fixed up the house and the chicken coop the best we could. The hens made eggs and some of them hatched.

One day, Papa built a secret door by the old stove in the corner of the kitchen and dug a little room out of the dirt below. He said, "You climb down in here if we ever have any visitors." Papa told me many times that men would do awful things to me if they ever found me. One time I asked him what that meant, and he told me that it didn't matter and that there were some things little girls shouldn't know no matter how bad things got in the world.

I remember the darkness and the cold and the smell of dirt around my face.

Down in my secret room, I waited for the men to leave but they didn't.

I wanted to get up and do something, but I didn't. I just stayed down there in the dark with Marilyn. She liked it down there. I think it made her feel safe.

"Shhh-shhh-shhhh," I thought, but I didn't dare say anything. "We must be brave now."

I brought Marilyn closer to me and held Papa's hatchet tight. Neither one of us made a sound—not when we heard one of the men say, "Woooo-eeee! We got him!" Not when we heard the men clomping around inside the house and going through everything Papa and I owned. Not when they tipped over the old iron stove and I could smell their bodies right over my head. Like onions and dirt. Not when they were dragging my Papa outside into the grass. Not even when we heard them busting around in the chicken coop and the hens clucked and clucked and I know Ricky kicked at their shins but it wasn't long before they were all quiet again.

After a while, it got even darker and colder in my secret room because night time was coming and the sun was going down. Then I had to pee, and I knew I couldn't go anywhere outside to do it so I held it as long as I could before I just went right there all over myself. Marilyn did too, except hers was an awful sticky ick that got all over my hands and smelled bad.

I could hear the men outside talking and laughing. It was a bad sound, like cold wet socks. One of them said they should build a fire and then I could hear them peeling wooden pieces off of the house. Through the spaces between the floorboards, I could see glowing and hear the crackling and smell the smoke coming up from the burning wood. And then I could smell the cooking chicken and my stomach woke up. Then I smelled another kind of cooking that was not at all like chicken. And my stomach remembered it was hungry again and started to growl. I hated myself for being so hungry and I hated the men for what they had done and I began to cry. I cried as quiet as I could, for as long as I had to.

I think I slept.

I remember my dream.

I was outside the old farmhouse, because I could see Papa out past the tall weeds by the chicken coop at the chopping block. Except it was different this time because he wasn't holding a chicken down on the oak stump. It was my Mama. I could hear her crying, and her shoulders were bouncing up and down like mine do when I fall down and hurt my knees. Papa was holding the hatchet.

"Why, Papa, why?" I said and I started to cry too. When Mama and Papa heard me, they turned their heads toward the sound of my crying and their eyes were swelled up and they looked so sad.

In my dream I could see my Mama's face, and it was just like the last time I saw her and she was so pretty but some of the skin was curled up and burned like a hot dog on the grill and one of her arms was black and pinched up tight against her side like it would never move again.

I didn't want to see that part, but I saw everything. And the world shook and grew up out of the ground because we were back home in the city, and the big tall buildings burned all around us farther than I could see down every street, and I felt the hot on my face and it burned away my tears. I could hear people screaming everywhere and glass breaking. Police sirens and women crying. I think the sky caught fire.

"It's O.K. sweetheart. Don't be afraid," said Mama to me, then she looked up at Papa and said, "You have to go, Clint."

"I know what they'll do to you when they find you. I won't let them," said Papa.

"Then don't let them. I can't do it for myself," said Mama, and the chopping block started on fire and both Papa and Mama began to burn there together.

"Oh, honey, I can't, I can't, I can't," said Papa, but I knew he made up his mind already that he was going to listen to Mama because he raised his big hand up high above his head just like he always does right before the hatchet comes down.

"Katie don't you watch this. Katie you look away. Katie close your eyes, baby, and don't you dare open them until I say," said Papa. I closed my eyes, but I knew. Papa said you can't think twice about it.

I remember his face watching me.

I could see the moonlight shining through the cracks in the floor and shining off the man's bald head. It was bumpy smooth all over and one of his eyes was gone. When he smiled at me, there were no teeth. I think Marilyn started clucking while I was asleep and the man must have heard the noise and came inside to see.

"What's this?" the man whispered down through the floor. "A little treat just for me, I think. Don't you make a sound now or you'll wake up my friend and we'll both have a go at you. Then we will eat you up."

I didn't make a sound, just like he said, and I watched him drag the knocked over stove off the floorboards. He had to push three times before he moved it. Then he reached for the handle to the door of the secret room and I held onto Marilyn and Papa's hatchet and my whole body was shaking I was so afraid. He opened up the door and when it creaked, he stopped and looked over his shoulder and put a finger up to his lips like "Shhhhh!" before he turned back to look at me again.

"Two little birds down in the hole?" whispered the man, bending down over the hole where I sat scrunched up, and he was close enough for me to smell the dead all over him. "This is a lucky place. Come here, now birdy." He reached down for us.

Marilyn listened to him and she went up to him. She flapped her wings into my eyes so I had to lean away from her and let her go up to where she wanted to be. My hair blew everywhere when Marilyn flew up into the man's face and his hands went up to his good eye and he howled and said all the words Papa told me never ever to say around other people.

I used Papa's hatchet on the man's legs and he screamed some more and fell down. He couldn't see anymore, and when he tried to grab at me, I buried the hatchet right in his shiny bumpy forehead and left it there. I didn't think twice about it.

Then I ran though I didn't know where I would go. I heard the other man say something behind me, but I kept running until I didn't hear him anymore.

Goodbye, house. Goodbye, Marilyn. Goodbye, Papa.

I remember the chopping block.

Papa's big arm came down with the hatchet and it made a thonk-sound against the oak and I watched Lucy's head roll off the side. Papa let go of Lucy and stepped back away from the chopping block then and she flapped her wings and kicked her legs around. There was blood, and I cried and hoped it wouldn't take her long to stop.

Papa left the hatchet buried in the oak stump and came over to wrap me up in his arms. "See? Now that's a good girl. Tell me why we give them names, Katie."

"Goodbye, Lucy," I said.

Lucy stopped moving after a while, and forgot everything bad that had ever happened to her. She went to sleep and didn't dream. I hoped she could maybe forget some for me, too, and for Papa, and for the whole world too, because I knew we could never do it for ourselves.

# CHUMS

## *Doug Murano*

The first time Chad saw the sharp, grey triangle rise up from the lake's glassy surface, he tried to tell himself it was just another hallucination. It wasn't an unreasonable assumption. Irrational visions were nothing new for Chad. What had started as casual drug use on weekends two years ago had ended last month with a thirty-day detox stint at the fancy clinic in Sioux Falls his family had insisted he visit. Shaking, vomiting, and hallucinating through the darkest moments of withdrawal, he had seen some nasty things, indeed.

None of it measured up to watching a shark's fin rise up from the placid surface of Billy Schmidt's pond, though. As Chad floated in the soggy confines of his belly boat, hands gripping the cork handle of his fishing rod, flippered feet dangling through the leg holes into the murk below, he watched it cut a lazy wake between him and his companion, Tim, before it descended back below the surface. Like the tip of an iceberg come to life, the fin's benign appearance betrayed the existence of all the dangerous parts below.

Chad's legs curled up instinctively against the bottom of his canvas-covered float-tube. His toes retreated from the tips of his flippers. He thought of enormous, fanged creatures staring up at his skinny legs (and his more vulnerable parts) with dumb, animal hunger and shivered. He craned his neck around to check for any sign that Tim had witnessed it, too.

"You see that? Goddamn crappie the size of a dinner plate just broke me off," said Tim. He tucked his rod underneath his armpit and worked on baiting up again. "Better get started before you miss out on all the action."

Chad's sigh of relief cut a tunnel through the cloud of gnats that had congregated near his face. Tim hadn't seen the fin. And why would he have? This wasn't the ocean, it was a manmade lake in the middle of some jerk's pasture.

Local pariah Billy Schmidt hit the $100 million Powerball jackpot five years ago. Winning the money hadn't done much to change Billy's disposition, improve his standing in town, or refine his tastes but it had gone a long way toward creating a mystique about him. He'd kept the shack he'd grown up in, drove the same broken down Dodge Ram from the 60's, ate the same crummy T.V. dinners.

When it came to building his fishing hole, though, Billy spared no expense—which provided a clear enough picture of the man's priorities. He bought up a few sections of land and diverted river water to flood a large draw smack-dab in the middle of his land.

Half a mile long, twenty feet deep in places, mechanically aerated, and geothermally heated so that it never froze over in the winter, the pond represented different things to different people around town. For old men drinking the senior special coffee, it replaced the weather and aches as a major topic of discussion and speculation. For the younger ones, it served as a significant source of much-needed excitement. Quite a few of them tried to cozy up to Billy in vain attempts to buddy up enough to gain access to his pond, and the monster crappie, perch and bass rumored to be within. Others, like Chad and Tim, didn't bother with Billy and snuck in on their own.

Not even the wildest rumors about the place included sharks. Besides, it was fresh water. Sharks could only survive in salt water.

*You're just being a crazy junkie,* Chad thought.

He decided not to mention it—didn't want to reveal himself to be the fool he thought Tim suspected him of being and alienate himself from the last person in the county who'd still put up with him. It had been Tim's idea to go fishing, and Chad suspected his friend wanted to keep him occupied with wholesome pursuits. If Chad started raving about sharks in the pond, who knows Tim might do. At best, he might laugh it off as a joke. Then again, Tim may end the fishing early and spend the rest of the night attempting to convince him to clean up his act. Just as likely, he'd lose his temper and throttle Chad.

"You alright, buddy?" asked Tim, inspecting Chad like an old woman does a melon at a fruit stand.

"Yeah, fine."

He baited up, tossed his line in and forced his legs to straighten. He willed his toes to stretch out as far as they would go, and tried to concentrate on everything above the water.

"There you go. Won't be long before you tie into one like I did," said Tim.

Chad closed his eyes, slowed his breathing and relaxed. The good folks at the clinic had taught him a few tricks to keep his mind clear, to stay in the moment when the cravings took hold, or when the withdrawal symptoms overwhelmed him. He sank into himself, focused on an awareness of his breathing, and inhaled the sweet scent of freshly cut alfalfa drifting on the breeze. Somewhere, a red-winged blackbird called out a song that sounded like a swinging, rusty gate.

Chad opened his eyes to the fin, and a wake rippled behind it. A grey outline cut a path just below the surface. Chad was no expert on marine life, but he estimated the fin's owner measured a dozen feet or more in length. Its sleek body flexed back and forth, propelling the beast silently through the cool water. He caught a glimpse of an eye, a piece of coal set deep in a fleshy concrete. Then it submerged. Little waves created by the fish's motion lapped at his sides. He might have been able to chalk it up to his fried synapses again, if not for those little waves. They caused a slight wobbling of his belly boat, while tiny splashes echoed against the inside of his inner tube. It was enough to get Chad moving.

"We need to get off the pond," said Chad.

He paddled toward Tim, who'd tied on something large, judging by the vicious bend in his rod.

"What the hell are you talking about? From what I hear, Billy-boy's vacationing on the coast for another week." Tim cranked his reel. The line dragged and groaned.

"I'm not feeling so hot."

This got Tim's attention. He cranked up the drag to full tension, stopped reeling and held his rod high over his head. The fish on the end of his line continued struggling as the line danced in tight, trembling circles against the water.

"Man, are you jonesin'? This is bullshit, man. I finally get something big on the line and now you want to go?" Tim said.

"It's not that. You know I'm clean. Something just ain't right"

The tip of Tim's fishing rod surged down, and the line drew frantic figure-eights on the pond. Tim chuckled. Chad's eyes darted around.

"What? You looking for him? It's not like he's gonna come rolling up here in his pickup toting a shotgun. I told you—I heard he's out of town."

A snap and a twang then the bend went out of Tim's fishing rod.

"Aw, hell! I had him dead to rights, Chad! That one was meant for the wall, man! Why can't you just relax and feel happy to be float-tubing with your buddy?"

"Because there's a shark swimming around here, that's why."

A hateful expression flashed across Tim's face. He reeled up the slack in his line and reached into one of the canvas pouches on his float tube, searching for another rig.

"Look man, I'm trying here, but if you keep this shit up…I love you like a brother, but I can't watch you fall apart in front of me again. I won't do it."

"It's not drugs, dammit! I've seen it twice now. I don't know how it's here, but it is. We need to go."

"You go right ahead—"

Something bobbed up between them. It was a large mouth bass bit cleanly in two, just behind the dorsal fin. A bright, green jig protruded from its bottom jaw, and a short length of monofilament line trailed down into the water.

"Well, I'll be damned," said Tim.

"See what I mean? That shark bit it in two."

"I've seen it a million times. Big pike or Muskie can do this kind of thing. And I'll tell you something else. I've had just about enough of you."

Tim paddled up next to Chad. Then he reached over, grabbed Chad by the neck of his t-shirt and pulled him close. "You want to mess around in dreamland, be my guest, but get the hell out of my sight."

Chad's eyes widened as he watched the fin rise to the surface and approach Tim from behind. He squeaked out a scream.

The fin disappeared back down under the surface several feet behind Tim, and Chad could see the fish was preparing an ambush. He began to thrash against his friend's grip.

"I ought to hold your head under 'till you stop kicking and save your poor mama the heartbreak of watching you ruin yourself again," he said.

Tim's body jerked downward, pitching them both forward. Their float tubes nearly capsized before they bobbed back. Both of Chad's flippers popped off his feet. At the same time, a muffled sound, not unlike ripping paper, came from somewhere near Tim's waist. As his friend's baritone voice built up into a girlish shriek, Chad became vaguely aware that they were accelerating across the water, leaving a trail of burgundy foam in their wake. Chad dropped his fishing rod and beat his track-marked arms against Tim's face and neck. He couldn't get out of Tim's death grip.

"Oh God! Oh God! Save me!" said Tim, head and hands thrown skyward like a Baptist experiencing religious ecstasy.

What he was, in fact, experiencing was the severing of his right thigh and femur, just above the knee. He pulled Chad in close, pawed at his shoulders, grasped at the folds in his shirt. Despite the massive blood loss and shock, Tim's strength hadn't quite left him, and he attempted to boost himself out of the water. Chad saw the ragged stump of a thigh, and a white knob of bone winking from tattered remains of flesh.

He watched the shark's broad head poke up through the ragged seat of Tim's belly boat, saw its rows of serrated teeth clamp down on his crotch and haul him back downward. The float-tube's stubborn buoyancy bobbed him back up again. The color drained out of Tim's face and he loosened his hold on Chad's shirt.

He pushed himself away from the scene and kicked, but his lack of flippers nullified the effort. A loud pop punctuated the evening air. Tim's float tube deflated, and he fell from his perch into the lake. Tim reached out one last time, and his throat emitted a horrible gurgling sound. Then he slipped below the surface.

The shark's tail flipped up in excitement as it feasted on meaty chunks of warm flesh.

Chad bobbed near the middle of the lake, helpless and stranded. He could leave his float tube and take his chances swimming, or he could stay aboard, hope the thing had eaten its fill and wait to drift to shore. Neither choice presented much hope. The shark had left Tim's corpse and settled into a wide circle around Chad.

He heard the low rumble of an old diesel engine. A rusted truck lurched over the hill and stopped near the shoreline. He watched Billy Schmidt exit the driver's side and peer out toward the middle of the lake.

"Hey! Help me!" said Chad. He flailed his arms.

Billy reached into his back pocket and brought out a small pair of binoculars, which he pressed to his deep-set blue eyes.

"I'll be damned. I told you and your dumbass friend to stay off my property. Looks like Timmy got it good. Don't you move. Wait right there," Billy shouted.

Billy waddled back to the rear of his old Dodge and reached into the bed. Then he returned to shore with a shotgun, one of those fold-up camp chairs and the kind of fishing rod Rob Schneider and Richard Dreyfus used in *Jaws*. "You fuckers are all the same."

"What the hell are you doing?"

The shark's circles tightened around him in the stained water like an invisible noose.

"You ever hear of *Carrcharhinus leucas*? No, I'll bet you haven't. Most people call 'em bull sharks." Billy unfolded his camp chair and sat down.

"There's one out here with me! It just ate Tim!"

"You know what makes the bull shark special? They can survive in fresh water. One'll swim up the Mississippi every few years."

Billy dug through his tackle box, picked out a long steel leader and fixed it to the end of his line.

"Had three stocked in here a few weeks ago, but haven't been able to get one to rise to my bait, no matter what I do. Now, I want one of those sharks before winter comes. You, of all people, should understand the need to chase the dragon," said Billy.

"Come on, man. Be a pal and help me out."

Billy stretched in his chair, tipped his hat back and chuckled.

"Pal? Everybody in town wants to be my pal. 'Sides, it doesn't look like your pals fare very well. Tell you what, though. I may not need any more pals, but you can bet your ass you'll be my chum."

Billy baited his hook and threw out his line.

# SAVIOR, TEACH US SO TO RISE

## *Doug Murano*

"What is mankind's greatest sin?" asks The Preacher as he stalks across the raised platform. His heavy black shoes clomp against the wooden planks and leave a trail of dark hollows in the thick dust. His words echo off thin metal walls.

The venue could be an old barn or a machine shed—difficult to tell with any certainty—the windows have been boarded and taped over, and the only light emanates from four candelabras which flank the corners of the makeshift stage.

He waits a few heartbeats before he continues, allowing time for his congregation's vision to adjust to the low light. One hundred spectators sit ten apiece in ten wooden pews.

"Envy, wrath, lust, pride, greed, sloth, gluttony. Surely, you might answer, man's greatest sin stands among these," The Preacher continues, ticking each transgression off one by one with his long fingers, his voice dropping low and trailing off. Soft murmurs spread through the congregation.

"You would be right to condemn these sins, but they're not the reason man has fallen from the Lord's grace," he yells and thrusts his hands skyward. Everyone sits silent, bolt upright, facing forward. "None of these is why I come to you tonight, and certainly not why you have gathered here in our sanctuary despite the threat of imprisonment and persecution to commune with the Lord."

Seven years earlier, Brian Hurd stood in the kitchen of his family's two bedroom ranch home and tugged at his father's pant leg. Brian wore his favorite Saturday afternoon play clothes—a Minnesota Twins t-shirt and faded blue jeans. "Dad, Dad, Dad...DAD! Let's go ride bikes. I can go fast now," Brian said. He flashed his best let's-go-for-a-bike-ride-on-a-Saturday-afternoon-Dad smile.

Brian's father sipped on his fifth can of Bud, ready to drink until there wasn't any more. At only thirty, Dwayne felt used up. He had given up on any pretensions of a career years ago, had his nine-to-five jerked out from underneath his feet last spring, and had to deal with a son whom he suspected wouldn't ever know enough to pound sand in a rat hole. Dwayne had hoped for none of it, planned for none of it. But here it all was, tugging at his pant leg.

He met Brian's grin with a morose frown. "Brian, quit hanging on me. You're like a monkey on a barrel, always got your paws wrapped around the leg of my pants. Go on outside and play. Lucy, will you tell your boy to go outside and let me be?" Dwayne asked. He paced across the flower patterned linoleum that coated the kitchen and both bathrooms, toward the big green La-Z-Boy in the corner of the living room. Brian's sneakers squeaked as they dragged behind.

Brian's mother stood in the back yard and hung clothes out on the line to dry. It was probably too late in the year to hang them outside, and the late September chill in the air would make them take twice as long to dry, but she liked the way the sun made them smell. And even if she couldn't always count on Dwayne's unemployment check to cover the electric bill, she could count on the wind to dry her sheets, and Lucy Hurd knew that even in early fall, if the sun stayed out, her sheets would dry just fine.

"Brian, listen to your father," she muttered while clipping clothespins to the flapping white sheets.

"But you never come with me, Dad," Brian said, trying not to whine. Ever since his dad wheeled the 24-inch Huffy back from the Uncle Randy's Tool and Pawn last month, Brian had been so proud of it. He wanted his dad to be as proud of him as he was of his new bike. Brian had visions of his whole family riding down shady boulevards, smiling and pedaling, but that's not how it turned out, no not at all. As with almost everything else he did, if Brian was riding, he rode alone.

"Boy, I know you understand what comes next if you don't let go of my pant leg. LUCY!" Dwayne grumbled and hopped a few times, trying to dislodge Brian from the nook created by the backside of his knee. He tried to take another pull from his beer, but Brian's weight threw him off-balance, and he spilled a few drops over his bottom lip.

"Cock...sucking...little...LUUUUCYYYY!"

"Brian, listen to your father," said Lucy absently through the open window.

Brian held on too long to his father's leg. "You hear me, LET GO!" Dwayne said and cracked a backhand across the left side of his son's face, knocking him to the linoleum. Brian hopped up, grabbed his jacket from the coat rack beside the door and fought back tears as his chubby legs carried him outside toward the garage.

Lucy called out behind him as he ran across the brown, patchy lawn, a faint grey silhouette beyond the white sheets, "If you ride down by the river, be careful. And don't stop to talk to any of those Mexicans! And stay away from the Sixth Street Bridge!"

Brian barely heard her. He pedaled his 24-inch Huffy bike as fast as he could through an invisible slalom down the sidewalk, down the big hill to the river and the Fourth Street Dam, down through the cool September air, down past the rundown motels and the classic cars up on cinder blocks. Down past the other squat houses that smelled like soup and dryer sheets. Down.

"Indifference!" says The Preacher, his voice breaking, his hands up and trembling.

"Yes! Speak!" croaks an old man's tired voice.

"Indifference!" The Preacher repeats. His words bounce between the thick wooden crossbeams that hang high above them like empty ribs.

"Yes, Lord!" an old woman's voice clucks from the blackness.

"Indifference is man's greatest sin against God, and indifference is why you have come to me tonight," says The Preacher.

"Save us, Lord!" says a young man's high tenor.

"Yes, indifference. More than all the hate we can conjure, more than all the spite our frail human souls can manufacture, indifference! Indifference blinds us to the needs of our family and friends. Indifference drives us quietly apart to live separate lives, away from our wives, our brothers, our sons and daughters who sit lonely and lost just down the darkened hallway. It is the same indifference that led us to reject the plain and simple will of the Lord; to reject the gifts that he has given us. Even to reject wholesale the promise that our Savior Himself made and sealed in blood for each and every one of us," says The Preacher.

Somewhere, a woman quietly stifles wet, hitching sobs.

"There are so few, too few, who hear the call of truth, and fewer who heed that call. There are even fewer believers who have the piety and will to deliver God's promise to the world. All of you are here tonight on a divine mission of no less importance than to deliver God's grace and promise unto this broken, damned world. Nothing less than the salvation of mankind is at stake tonight. You seek the means to obey God's will and deliver the good news," says The Preacher who then nods.

Five hooded, robed figures emerge from the shadows behind him. Each carries a deep brass bowl. But unlike traditional offering plates which are empty when they reach the congregation, these shallow bowls are full— brimming with long, nondescript white envelopes. The hooded figures begin to pass the bowls amongst the seated congregation, and each member takes an envelope.

The crisp air felt good on the red side of Brian's face, and by the time he could hear the faint but steady rush of water flowing over the dam, his father's cruelty had faded from his mind.

Brian thought of the reassuring hum of his tires against the rough pavement, the sweet smell of the turning leaves, and how good it would feel someday, when he won his first big bike race.

"That's my boy!" Brian heard through the cheers inside his head, and the deep voice was his father's. Television and newspaper reporters shouldered in on each other, wanting to write down whatever he said, needing to chronicle whatever he did next.

Fourth Street Dam on the James River was a small spillway that slowed the James down long enough for the water treatment plant to feed Norah's taps and garden hoses. It was also one of the best fishing spots on the river for miles. When the fishing hit its peak in mid-April, you could go down to the dam any time of the day in the middle of the week and have a chance to meet almost any man in Norah.

By September, when the big fish stopped biting, the doctors and businessmen stopped playing hooky to pitch minnows. Most of the kids were gone, too, busy with schoolwork, friends and after-school activities. That left the Mexicans as Brian's parents (and most of Norah) thought and spoke of them. Most had arrived legally, but the good citizens of Norah assumed that if a person came to South Dakota who had brown skin and didn't speak English, he or she had probably spent some time swimming across the Rio Grande ducking border agents and taking jobs away from the hard-working, God-fearing white Americans who deserved them.

Brian braked on the rough sidewalk that ran parallel to Fourth Street along the top of the final gentle slope to the river. He could see a few Mexicans in green flannel shirts sitting along the concrete safety walls up close to the dam, casting spinners into the froth.

Brian sat up straight and puffed out his chest to show them all what a big boy he was. He hoped the sun caught the gleam off his shiny red bike. Brian pedaled along the sidewalk upstream, then downstream as fast as he could past a group of fishermen, admiring the whooshing sound his jacket made as it cut through the breeze. Brian pedaled upstream again, but this time when he turned on the juice to go downstream, he let out a "Whoooooooooeeeee!" The men looked up at Brian, frowned, and turned back to their discussion.

"Hey! Hey! Want to see how fast I can go on my new bike?" Brian said.

Nobody answered him.

He rode toward the bridge that lifts Sixth Street over the James. A young couple walked their chocolate Labrador retriever puppy as they made their way toward the dam. Brian yelled, "I got a new bike, wanna see how fast I can go?" He sped between them. The puppy went bananas and wrapped its leash around the young woman's legs, spilling her to the ground.

"Jesus, kid. What the hell's wrong with you?" said the young man as he helped his girlfriend up.

"Look! I don't need training wheels and I can go fast!" Brian said as he turned around and sliced a path between the couple again. The lab puppy sat down and started to howl.

"Are you fucking retarded?" said the young man, dodging out of the way.

"Shhhh! I'm fine. Look. I'm just fine. I don't think he knows any better," said the woman, unwrapping the leash from between her ankles.

For a moment she wanted to say something to him. Something like, "Yeah, I see how fast you can go. What's your name, little boy? Are you training for a race?" She wanted to tell him to be careful who he shows his bicycle to, because someday, she imagined, he's going to talk to the wrong person, and that made her feel sad. But she didn't say anything.

"I don't care..." began the man, but Brian lost the rest to the roar of the wind and the perpetual librarian's shush of the river water. He pedaled down the sidewalk again, downstream toward the dark overhang of the Sixth Street Bridge.

"And what is that good news?" asks The Preacher after everyone takes an envelope.

"Victory over death!" responds the congregation.

"Victory over death. He promised His children victory over that cold, dark lasting oblivion into which every child of God must someday enter. And we saw that promise begin to bear fruit upon the world!"

"Victory over death!" shouts the congregation.

"Indeed, you are sent forth to again bring victory over death to your fellow man—to make good on the promise of God the Father and His Son Jesus Christ. We few here tonight are the vessels of His purpose, sent to save our brothers and sisters from the corruption and indifference that has spread once again through our midst. And fear not, children of God. You need not go alone. Remember, the power of God will be with each of you as you go. What is the good news?"

"Victory over death!"

Brian peered into the shadows beneath the concrete Sixth Street Bridge and saw a figure standing there, the dark silhouette of a girl, perhaps twelve years old. To Brian's young eyes, she looked like a woman. The girl stared from the shadows into the roiling water rushing between the river's muddy banks.

He slowed his bike to a crawl and then dragged the toes of his sneakers along the bumpy, broken sidewalk to stop. He remembered his mother's warning: "And stay away from the Sixth Street Bridge!"

He had every intention of turning his bike around and riding back up the hill to his house, content with another fine (if somewhat unsatisfactory) day's ride when the girl turned her head and looked at him. Something in her gaze stopped him. Loneliness filled those pale blue eyes, and a desire lurked there as well. He felt a deep wanting in the way she looked at him. That singular, focused attention enticed Brian in a way that he would never grow up to understand.

The living corpse—one of the first of millions—began to shamble toward Brian, her dull lips parted in anticipation, her arms outstretched with yearning.

Brian watched her grasp for him, and although her appearance made him uneasy, he reached out to her in kind. She stared at Brian like he was the only thing in the world—like those people in his dreams who screamed his name and hung on his every move. Thinking of this, Brian said the first thing that came to his mind.

"Do you want to see my new bike? I can go fast."

By the time it occurred to Brian to scream, the worst was finished. He pushed the dead girl away, and she rolled down the embankment into the rust-colored water then floated downstream without a sound.

Brian lay on the ground and noticed a widening pool of blood. It expanded around him, and ran into the cracks of the hot cement. The color matched the red paint of his new bike, which created the illusion that he, along with it, melted under the sun like a discarded ice cream cone. Brian closed his eyes and smiled at the thought.

"Few expected the Messiah to arrive into the world, born to a poor family in a cold stable. But He did. Similarly, we did not expect the Lord's promise to arrive as it did. Closed by indifference our eyes did not see and our hearts did not comprehend. We here stand among the few who have the humility to accept. For what, in arrogance...in hubris...INDIFFERENCE did humanity insult and reject with bombs and bullets and quarantine?" says The Preacher.

"Victory over death!" responds the congregation in unison.

The Preacher pauses to collect himself, his knees locked, his gaunt frame trembling.

"What did we stifle and destroy and fence off and eradicate in defiance of the will of the Lord?" erupts The Preacher, producing an unfolded newspaper in his outstretched hand. The front page headline (dated two months before) reads "GOVERNMENT HEALTH AGENCIES CONFIRM WALKING DEAD PLAGUE ENDS AT LAST!"

"Victory over death! Victory over death! Victory over death!" responds the congregation, their voices rising toward equal measures of despair and jubilation.

"It comes tonight!" says The Preacher.

The same hooded figures that dispersed the brass bowls emerge again from the shadows, but this time they're dragging what appears to be a large wooden post wrapped in a black sheet. They deposit the parcel upon the stage in front of The Preacher. Something stirs.

Now The Preacher produces a long curved blade. He kneels down beside the dark package and begins to cut away the ropes binding the sheet to the wooden post and to the writhing object beneath. The congregation's chant dissolves into a random spilling of excited voices, unintelligible, animalistic. The Preacher raises his hand, silencing his flock.

He waits. And waits.

"It was said that there were none left in the world such as you are about to see. It was said that we had turned them away forever. But behold! Enduring proof of the promise!"

The congregation erupts anew into chants of "Victory over death!"

"You are so special," whispers The Preacher who kneels down and leans close to the form under the black sheet. "Yours truly is the face of God."

He removes the black sheet with a flourish. Before him lies a small figure tied to the post, hands bound above its head, feet and legs secured with thick braided rope.

There are few recognizable features left on the desiccated face but exposed teeth and jawbones, flaking skin and the crusty remains of one eyeball that sits like a dried plum in the socket.

A Minnesota Twins t-shirt hangs in filthy rags below the small figure's ruined face.

Lucy watched Brian stagger up the hill as he returned home, bloody and without his bike—he never would have lost his bike. Dropping her laundry basket, charging through the damp clothes hanging on the line, she moved with surprising speed toward Brian panting, "Oh, my baby! Oh, Brian, oh my baby, have those Pickett boys been at you again?" It took Brian's small teeth two attempts before they pierced through Lucy's thick neck and tore out her throat, cutting short her cries of shock and disbelief. Her chunky hands rose instinctively to the gaping wound in her neck while her racing heart sprayed crimson arcs between her fingers and into the crisp September air. As she fell to the ground, her lips mouthed the words "Oh my" and then she was gone.

The same might have happened to Dwayne if the squeaking of his dead son's sneakers against the yellow flower patterned linoleum floor hadn't woken him from his afternoon nap. When Brian rushed him, Dwayne managed to kick the boy down the stairs and lock him in the canning cellar. Dwayne ran out of the house to the back yard, cursing blue thunder and looking for Lucy, but all he found were bloody sheets fluttering in the constant prairie wind and a trail of red, matted grass headed in the direction of downtown Norah.

It took two weeks before Dwayne could bring himself to open the cellar door—the day the news reports finally confirmed it was happening everywhere, even though nobody knew what it was, where it had come from, or if it could be cured. By the end of the next week, he had devised a way to safely immobilize Brian. By the end of that month, the airwaves went to static, and the fragmented attempts at evacuation ended.

By then, many of the "stumblers" had moved on from Norah and had joined up with the larger hoards that migrated to urban areas, although groups of them would often follow Dwayne's warmth and living scent to the house. Then they would bang on the windows and siding until he made them stop.

The day he had to crush his brother, Scott's skull with a cinder block, Dwayne opened his old confirmation Bible for the first time in fifteen years. Soon after that, terrified, utterly alone and convinced that God was punishing him for his failures as a husband and father, he retreated down to the canning cellar, and spent hours hiding in the darkness, eating Lucy's pickled beets and canned apples by the jarful and praying with Brian by candle light.

That was the first time in his life Dwayne ever felt any real kinship with his son, a feeling that grew little by little. Then one day, and he couldn't remember exactly when—but he could remember on that day crouching on the dirt floor in a dark corner of the canning cellar, reading about the promise of resurrection, praying silently with Brian and listening to shuffles and hoarse moans through the floorboards above his head—it felt right to pray to Brian.

Time passed. Dwayne lived on, and a thought germinated in his mind: despite his years spent living in wickedness and indifference, God had chosen to show him the Truth. Brian was a gift...a promise to the world. Dwayne was that gift's custodian. The Lord had seen fit to give him another chance to appreciate the gifts in his life. Eventually, he found a survivor who came to agree. They found another. And another.

Propped up in front of the congregation, what's left of Brian's face snaps its white jaw open and shut in hunger. The remnant of Brian's voice box hisses and wheezes in a sick approximation of a little boy's cry. His rotten eardrums vibrate when a deep voice whispers "That's my boy," and the voice Brian's body hears is his father's. Brian writhes, and his loose flesh strips off in dry bits.

"Approach, and receive the gift," says Dwayne addressing his flock while using his knife to slice a strip of black, reeking flesh from Brian's arm—and so they do. One by one, they approach the makeshift altar and kneel in reverence. Some weep in ecstasy as they raise their hands, open their mouths and accept bits of flesh, not unlike strings of beef jerky, upon their tongues.

One by one they come to worship and receive the now and forever nine-year-old Brian Hurd. When each of the one hundred members of the congregation has been served—infected—they are again seated.

"Indifference is the greatest sin against the Lord. With what we do tonight, we choose not allow it to prevail!" says Dwayne.

The members of the congregation open their envelopes. One man removes an airline ticket to London. A middle-aged woman removes a ticket to Paris. A third person, a young man who couldn't be older than nineteen, discovers he's scheduled to visit Sydney, Australia tomorrow morning.

"May your hand be outstretched to all you meet," says Dwayne, standing over his son, with his own arms extended and spread wide, delivering the final benediction to his congregation. "Go forth now," he says—and so they do. Every last one of them has a plane to catch.

The last person exits the sanctuary, and Dwayne cuts the ropes that hinder Brian's movement. When the last rope lies severed on the dusty platform, Brian stumbles forward over the thick braids coiled around his feet and reaches out to the warmth of the living body before him. Brian wraps his arms around his father's leg, and this time Dwayne doesn't curse, doesn't try to kick the boy away. Instead, he pulls his son close, saying "What do you say about taking a nice long walk, just you and me? I want you to show me how fast you can go."

Later, Dwayne follows Brian through the doors and out of the sanctuary (a rusted sheet metal tractor shed on the outskirts of town it turns out). As he walks with his son out into the moonlight, his heart is finally still.

# FIREBOOMERS

## *Doug Murano*

*What a cluster-fuck.*

Officer Hammond crossed the threshold of the doorway into the machine shed. Driving out to the country to find an old man who'd worked himself to death in the July heat was one thing, but the smell coming in waves from inside the metal structure suggested a wild animal problem, and that was something else entirely. He drew his pistol and moved forward.

Hammond couldn't call for backup. In a town the size of Cherry, he was the sheriff, the deputy, and the goddamned dog catcher. Besides, most of the town was already half-cocked at the Independence Day street dance. That meant yet another busy night, another holiday he'd have to miss.

The day's last light filtered through the small, rectangular windows spaced along the tin shed's long walls. Hammond's flashlight cut an alley of daylight through the spacious blackness that didn't reveal much-- just some dusty cardboard boxes, broken lawn mowers, and a few moldy straw bales.

Flashes of green and red seared through the windows, followed a few seconds later by a loud crackling sound. The sun wasn't even down yet, but the good people of Cherry didn't waste any time when it came to celebrating the nation's birthday.

Before he left town, Hammond promised his son that this year would be different, that he'd be there this time to watch "the fire boomers." If he didn't get himself in gear, Davie would be crushed. Again. He decided to perform a quick sweep of the shed and then scoot his boots down the road. The heat in there had started to choke him out. And then there was that smell—the sickening sweet-and-sour of death and something underneath, like the lion cages at the zoo.

He stopped when he saw a human form on the floor a dozen feet in front of him.

"Well, shit," said Hammond. He approached the old man's corpse, which lay face down in the dirt. Pools of congealing blood flanked his midsection like obscene wings.

Kneeling down, he grabbed the body by the shoulder and wrenched it onto its back. What was left of Miles Brody's abdominal cavity reminded Hammond of the cattle mutilations he'd seen over the past few weeks. It was a growing problem nobody in Cherry wanted to acknowledge with more than threats toward the local coyote population. Whatever had disemboweled the old guy had also plucked his eyes out of the sockets and sliced off his nose, leaving only his mouth intact, which hung open in mute protest.

Red and blue lights blossomed outside and glinted off the old man's teeth. Soft reports followed.

That monkey-house smell grew stronger still. Ragged breaths filled the air behind Hammond. Then, a sound like someone pulling a garden hose across dry ground.

He barely had time to turn around before it was on him, ripping into his insides just the way it had done to

Miles Brody. His only shot went wide before the thing reached one of its malformed limbs to knock the pistol away. Then the other hand fell to the ground, still clutching its flashlight. Thus disarmed, Hammond screamed and battered the thing's moist skin with his gushing stumps as the creature continued its deadly work. Wet sounds, like a serving spoon moving through his wife's famous macaroni salad (which she brought to the pot luck earlier in the afternoon), echoed off the shed's thin walls.

More colorful blossoms filled the windows when the thing pinned him to the dry ground and brought its smooth, broad, glistening face up close to Hammond's. As he faded into oblivion, Hammond watched little stars—blue, green, red and yellow—cavort and dance deep within the thing's vast black eyes.

*I made it to the fire boomers, Davie*, he thought. *I made it this year.*

# PAVEMENT ENDS

## *Doug Murano*

Jacob counted the seconds and prayed for the landscape to change. He watched the vast, brown expanses of grassland and cattle pastures creep by with the sluggishness of tectonic plates. The occasional billboard for Wall Drug advertised "free ice water." He saw a pronghorn buck chewing without enthusiasm on a mouthful of sage. *Even the animals are bored.*

"I know a good game, kids," said Lurane, digging through her purse. "See how many license plates from different states we pass. Write them down on these."

Her golden earrings jangled as she leaned over the Buick's front seat and handed click-pens and stationery from their latest hotel stay to Jacob and his little sister, Olivia.

"Booooring," said Olivia.

Jacob leaned forward and took the pens and stationery. Then he shot a menacing glare at Olivia. She was always such a pain on road trips, and he'd wanted to fly back to Denver from Sioux Falls this year. His mother said Olivia was still too young to travel alone by jet without an adult, and their grandfather insisted on making the drive. They planned to stop for the night in Rapid City.

"I'm with Liv," said Henry. He leaned back as he guided the Buick, one knobby, arthritic hand draped over the wheel. "We haven't passed another car for seventy miles. That's the whole idea of avoiding the interstate. No road construction, either. What do we say, Jake?" he asked, gunning the engine up. The abrupt shift in momentum jolted Lurane, who plopped back down in her seat with a huff.

"South Dakota has two seasons: winter and road construction," Jacob parroted, smiling in spite of himself. His grandpa's jokes were almost as old as he was, but that was part of the appeal.

"Why don't you kids try writing about something out there? Maybe you'll see a legendary jackalope," said Henry.

Jacob was coming up on twelve and had grown out of believing in the jackalope. What was *actually* out there didn't interest him much. His mind returned to dark thoughts. It was easy for that to happen—feeling so alone. Driving out here, you might not see another soul for hours at a time. Cell phone reception was spotty at best and nonexistent at other times. It felt like anything at all could happen out here. Anything at all.

To the west, thunderheads bruised the sky, dumping thick curtains of rain on the flat, dry land. Bright flashes of lightning bloomed deep within the clouds. The heavy sheet of falling rain made it impossible to see anything beyond.

"Are there gonna be tornadoes, Grammy?" asked Olivia. She had become obsessed with the fear of being sucked into the sky ever since she caught a tornado season documentary on The Weather Channel a few weeks ago. Olivia had already sketched a few ragged-looking funnel clouds on her stationary paper.

"No, sweetheart nothing bad like that. Everything's fine." She turned to grandpa and sighed theatrically.

"Nothing wrong with a little rain," he said.

For the first time in hours, Jacob saw vehicles on the road—two, in fact, coming toward them in the adjacent lane. They looked small in the distance as they exited the storm's impenetrable darkness, materializing as if from nowhere. He could tell that they were moving fast by the rate at which they seemed to grow.

"Oh, look kids! Better get your pens and paper ready," said Lurane.

Soon, the first car had driven close enough to tell the make—an old, green GMC heavy-duty ranch pickup with a cattle guard on the grille. There was no front license plate, but that wasn't uncommon for the area. The truck's windshield wiper blades flapped across the broad glass like crazy, even though it wasn't raining. The driver hunched low over the wheel. Jacob could see the green nub of his John Deere cap, and little else. He didn't wave, as so many of the locals did out here. Instead, he laid hard on his horn when he sped by them. A wave of rushing air made the Buick shimmy on its shocks as the big truck whipped by.

"Hope you get to wherever you're going," said Henry.

Jacob unbuckled his seatbelt and turned to look out the back window at the license plate. He noticed two things: that the truck sported South Dakota plates (a slight disappointment), and also that the back bumper had somehow come loose. Part of it dragged behind on the rough pavement, creating an impressive shower of sparks.

"Wonder what got under his bonnet," said Henry.

"He was probably trying to avoid the w-e-a-t-h-e-r," said Lurane, spelling out the last so as not to alarm Olivia.

"I think he got into an accident or something. His rear end is all messed up," said Jacob.

"His rear end was all mess-ied up," repeated Olivia. She said "rear end" to herself again, and giggled.

"Oh, dear. I hope they're all right," said Lurane.

Henry chuckled, and his wide shoulders bounced. "I've seen worse than that driving around here, Jake. Those old ranchers run 'em at full tilt until there ain't much left," he said.

The second vehicle followed close behind. Riding jacked-up off the road, with its intimidating black hulking form and massive tires, it resembled the kind of monster truck Jacob had seen a few times at the state fair.

The last bit of daylight glinted off the chrome bumpers and running boards. The windows, even the windshield it seemed, were tinted too dark for him to see inside the cab. Unlike the GMC, this truck had a front license plate. Jacob got a glimpse of it as the truck accelerated past with a roar that sounded like what God giving a raspberry would sound like. Another rush of air rocked the Buick, and Henry muttered something under his breath.

Its license plate was plain, bright red with bold white lettering. Jacob had never seen one like it before. He couldn't be completely sure, but, instead of a random series of letters and numbers, he thought the license plate read: NOWHR. He jotted down the letters, puzzled.

"Grammy, what does this mean?" he asked, turning around and handing his pad over the seat to Lurane.

"People with money to throw away get special plates sometimes to show off," she said. "There isn't enough space to write words out, so it's missing a few letters. I think it says 'NOWHERE.' This man must have a sense of humor about where he lives."

Nowhere. As in, middle of. Jake thought it would have been funny under different circumstances. There was no telling, really, why the trucks were speeding down the highway. People were strange out here. He couldn't shake the feeling that the driver in the first truck was running away from something. Maybe it was the storm, like his grandmother had suggested. But maybe not.


A few miles later, the rain started. It all seemed to come down out of the sky at once, like buckets and buckets of movie rain. Jacob thought moving into the storm felt like sliding through thick, velvet curtains into another world. The late afternoon disappeared into midnight. Great arcs of lightning spread across the sky in patterns like breaking glass. Puddles formed in the shallow ruts that had been worn into the asphalt. Henry flipped the headlights on and turned the wipers up.

"Henry, slow us down a little. We don't want to hydroplane into the ditch," said Lurane, bracing against the dash with one hand and clutching her armrest with the other.

"Just sit tight. Nobody's hydroplaning anywhere. I have to concentrate on the road. I'd appreciate some quiet," he said, leaning forward. He let off the gas and cranked the wipers up. It didn't do much good. As soon as the blades made a pass, another thick wave of water obscured the windshield.

They crept down the highway for a few miles like that--beams and wipers on high, everyone a little afraid. Nobody said a word until Lurane saw the approaching yellow reflection of a highway construction sign.

"Pavement ends," she read aloud. "There goes your theory about avoiding the road work, Henry. Does that mean we'll be driving down a dirt road in the rain?"

"When there are just two lanes of highway like this, they usually do them both at once. Just a little stretch of gravel up ahead," said Henry. Up the road, a dim white light glowed against the rain-soaked blackness. To their collective surprise, they also saw two sets of tail lights glowing red near the stop. "I think I see someone up there," he said, beginning to decelerate. He slowed the Buick to a stop a few feet behind the second car's tail lights.

In between wiper blade passes, Jacob got a sense of the scene ahead. The road construction station consisted of a large propane lamp held up high on a metal post, a green port-o-john and what appeared to be a very rugged-looking woman in a dark slicker who sat underneath a wide canopy on a black director's chair. Rain dropped from the canopy's edges in sheets. The worker held a sign in her hand that said "STOP." Jacob knew from experience that the other side said "SLOW," and when it was time for them to drive down the one-lane path ahead, she would turn it around and give them the nod.

"What do we do now, Grampy?" asked Olivia.

"Well, sweetheart, we wait until they tell us we can go. If we go too soon, we'll run into trouble because there will be other cars coming down the same way we want to go. We don't want that, do we Liv?" said Henry.

"No, Grampy. But we can't stay too long here," said Olivia.

"Why's that?" asked Lurane.

"I have to go potty," said Olivia, crossing her legs at the knees. "Bad."

"Liv, we asked you if you had to go back in Pierre," said Jacob.

"But I dint have to goooo then."

Up ahead, flashing yellow lights appeared. The worker turned her sign around to read "SLOW" as the highway truck came into view. With a U-turn, the truck positioned itself in front of the lead car, a maroon sedan. As soon as the sedan and the highway truck crept into the rain and out of view, the woman with the sign spun it around again to read "STOP." The remaining cars crept forward and then sat idling. Jacob was sure he saw a red license plate just above the guide vehicle's back bumper.

The rain pounded the Buick's metal roof in a sustained drum roll. Since they'd advanced, he could get a slightly better look at the woman. She was a monstrous, hulking piece of femininity. Her face bunched up in a constant sneer. Jacob didn't like looking at her. In fact, looking at her made him want to get out of the car and run.

"Must want to be extra careful because of the weather," said Henry. "Normally, they'd let us all go at once if there wasn't anyone else coming. It'll be awhile. You're going to have to be brave and hold it," he said.

"But Grampy!" said Olivia.

"That's enough, Olivia," said Henry. "It'll be quicker than you think."

But it wasn't. In fact, according to the digital clock embedded in the Buick's radio, an hour passed before Olivia piped up again.

"Potty, Grampy," said Olivia.

"Well, this is ridiculous," said Lurane. "Nobody else has even come from the other way. What are they doing up there?"

"I know," Henry said grasping his wife's wrinkled hand.

"Why have you got to be so darned stubborn?" asked Lurane.

"You wouldn't have married me otherwise," he said.

None of this felt right. Jacob had been thinking of the fleeing man in the GMC and the black truck in pursuit. Did they witness an escape earlier? The words: *We have to get out of here*, raced through his mind. But his grandfather was no longer in the mood for dispute. "I wonder if the others are getting sick of sitting here," was all Jacob could manage.

He didn't wait long for an answer. The driver of the blue Chevy SUV ahead of them hopped out of the cab and into the rain. He was a short, fat, balding man, probably in his forties, and dressed in standard yuppie vacation attire: khaki cargo shorts and an ill-fitting polo shirt.

Jacob watched him march over to the highway worker with the self-important stride he immediately recognized as being the walk of SOMEONE IN CHARGE. He'd seen that walk in a lot of banks and on more than a few golf courses.

The man stopped a few paces in front of the canopy and began speaking to the worker. He gestured wildly and wiped water off of his face in brusque strokes every few seconds. The sheets of water falling over the windshield and the accompanying wiper sweeps created an unnerving strobe effect to his motions. *Swipe.* Now, he throws his hands up in the air. *Swipe.* Now, he points back at his large vehicle. *Swipe.* Now, he leans forward like someone who is used to getting his way. *Swipe.* Now, the construction worker gestures up the road and nods her wide head.

Mr. Yuppie began to stomp his feet and scream. Splashes flanked his thighs, pumping like pistons. A few of his words even carried over the driving rain: *fucking, incompetent, vacation.*

In the next moments, everything unraveled. Jacob watched it all unfold in a slideshow-like presentation.

The woman stands up. *Swipe.* She reaches back as if to punch the man in his considerable gut. *Swipe.* Her hands are buried in his midsection. The man doubles over her forearms and his mouth contorts into a wide "O" shape. *Swipe.* His guts lay in a pile on the ground in front of him. Mr. Yuppie stares down in disbelief. *Swipe.* Mr. Yuppie lies sprawled out on the wet highway, opened up wide from waist to collar bone. *Swipe.* Blood, mixed with rain water, flows down the slope of the pavement into the ditch. The woman sits in her chair and stares at Jacob. Aside from the bright liquid covering the front of her slicker, it's as if nothing happened.

Lurane screamed. Olivia shrieked. Henry coughed.

All Jacob could do was sit and stare as whoever was in the passenger seat of the Chevy hopped the center console, shifted the vehicle into gear and slammed on the gas. The SUV disappeared behind the sheets of rain. Lightning flashed, and the shadow of something massive moved in the obscure distance, came down on the Chevy with a massive thud. A tire bounded back toward the port-o-john before coming to rest in the ditch.

The construction woman smiled at Jacob, her sharp teeth glinting against the cold propane light. When she removed her slicker, her skin sloughed off with it and fell to the saturated earth in a single, floppy sleeve. Underneath this covering was a tumor-ridden ruin of a form. Leathery wings sagged from its shoulders. Stubby tentacles sprouted and writhed from everywhere--elbows, knees, even from the pointed tips of its withered, vestigial breasts, where nipples should have been. Those, she used to wave at Jacob. Finally, he screamed.

"Oh my God! Oh my God!" said Lurane, clutching her own shoulders.

Olivia wailed as a dark stain spread across her denim shorts.

"Hang on!" said Henry. He jerked the shifter into reverse and hit the gas, sending fountains of water sailing in front of the Buick. Weaving back and forth, they moved away from the highway station and the terrible things ahead. Then they slammed into something solid. Jacob turned to look out the back window.

Behind them, a large, jacked-up truck idled with a low rumble--one Jacob recognized. Just below the front bumper, a bright red license plate with "NOWHR" in bold white lettering. *This is where we are: Nowhere.*

Strapped to the hood was the farmer from the fleeing GMC, or what was left of him. His head rested like a hood ornament, front and center. The man's mouth hung open in a pained grimace, and his dead eyes bulged wide with terror. Rain collected in and seeped from both. He still had on his John Deere cap. The dead man's cheeks jiggled when the driver of the black pickup gunned his engine and the vehicle lurched forward. The front bumper nudged the Buick and began to slowly push the car toward the massive shadows that shifted behind the veil of heavy rain.

Cool air swept through the car as Olivia opened her door, bailed out, and ran behind the port-o-john.

"No, Liv! Come back here," Henry said, throwing the car into park and exiting the vehicle. He rounded the corner of the toilet in a stiff jog.

"Don't leave us here, Henry!" said Lurane.

Seconds later, the port-o-john blasted up from the ground like something exploded underneath it, revealing a cowering Olivia crouched low to the ground. Two enormous segmented legs, which ended in cruel, barbed pinchers, surged from the hole below. The first one grabbed her and pulled her into the pit without a sound. Another grabbed Henry by the leg and tossed him skyward. It snatched his tumbling form out of the air and pulled him sideways into the hole. Jacob watched in horror as his grandpa tried to brace himself against the edges of the pit. A loud crack punctuated the rainfall as his spine broke, and Henry folded in two. The claws disappeared back down the hole.

"Don't you dare leave this car," Lurane said, turning to Jacob. She didn't see the monstrous highway woman flanking her window, and Jacob didn't have time to warn her. Thick, clawed hands crashed through the glass, grabbed Lurane around the throat and pulled her, gurgling, from the car. Jacob saw massive, bat-like wings spread across the windows. Then he saw his grandmother's body, clutched in the thing's arms, breeze upward and disappear into the sky.

The Buick continued its slow skid toward whatever gigantic, malformed creatures cast the shadows up ahead. Red, juicy pieces landed on the windshield and slid slowly downward, leaving dark trails down the glass.

Alone in the Buick, skidding toward horrors beyond his comprehension, Jacob sobbed. He knew he wasn't going home, and he wondered if all storms on the South Dakota prairie had the potential to spawn monsters. He didn't think so. This was something else altogether—not just a storm. There was no getting away.

Wiping his eyes, he bailed over the front seat and behind the wheel. It was a stretch for him to see over the dash and reach the pedals, but he only needed to make sure the car went straight enough to stay on the road. Jacob shifted the Buick into drive and stepped on the gas. Looking into the rearview mirror, he saw that the "NOWHR" truck had stopped pushing and sat idly behind him, waiting. Jacob felt a bump as the Buick's tires passed over Mr. Yuppie's gutted form.

Accelerating wildly, Jacob drove past dozens of wrecked car bodies, over mutilated, half-eaten corpses strewn across the road, weaving between the massive, thrashing insect and reptilian forms that reached out for him. Their scaly limbs scratched against the Buick's hull. It wasn't long before the pavement *did* end, just like the sign promised. He sped on through the downpour anyway, deep into Nowhere.

Jacob counted the seconds and prayed for the landscape to change.

# GHOST SOUP

## *Adrian Ludens*

Truman Bonner grunted from the effort as he backed down the stone steps leading to the Chinese laundry tunnels beneath Deadwood. His son, Isaac, followed. Between them, hogtied and drenched in sour sweat, writhed the lunatic prospector, Clarence Conroy. Their captive would have been howling in protest if not for Truman's dirty bandanna wadded up in his mouth. The pair hauled Clarence down into the stone passageway. The flickering oil lanterns nailed to support beams cast just enough light to assure him that he hadn't gone blind.

As they moved along, Truman wrestled with guilt over involving his son in such a ghastly endeavor. Yet he had to admit that Isaac had been through worse. In fact, his son seemed to gain inner strength from their strange adventures. Isaac showed more bravery and presence of mind than any other fourteen-year-old Truman had ever met. Despite the twinges of guilt, there was no one he trusted more in situations like this.

Truman knew these tunnels better than any other white man in the Black Hills. They afforded the Chinese laundry workers the shortcuts they needed to transport linens without having to contend with the muddy, crowded streets of the booming mining town, but the rugged cowboy was also well aware of the opium dens secreted in the warren of underground passageways.

Here also was where the nun Mary Agnes Gwyn was covertly cloistered. Her papal enclosure was only a crude cell, its grillwork made of heavy iron bars, all of it shrouded in perpetual darkness.

It was two years ago this month, Truman realized, that he and Sheriff Seth Bullock had made their solemn vow to ensure that Mary Agnes Gwyn never saw the sun again. They had worked with certain members of the Chinese-immigrant community to facilitate the building of this secret prison. The memories flooded back as he retraced his steps.

*"Damn it!" Sheriff Bullock pounded one palm with his fist. "Where in hell is that Indian?"*

*"He'll be here, I trust him." Truman gazed down the darkened passage. The two men stood waiting in the damp, earthy tunnel.*

*"He damn well better be." Bullock growled. "Sister Mary Agnes isn't going to last much longer. If this doesn't work, may God have mercy on us all."*

*"And if it does work?"*

*The sheriff seemed to consider, then looked Truman square in the eye. "May God have mercy on us all either way."*

Still carrying Clarence, Truman and Isaac shambled along a deceptive series of turns until they finally reached a dead end. Truman pressed one of the stones and part of the wall receded. The cowboy lit an oil lantern he found hanging from a spike just inside the revealed entrance and held it aloft. He looped the fingers of his free hand under the length of rope binding the prospector's wrists and lifted. The rope bit at Truman's palm as the trio descended farther into the depths of the earth. The air chilled and became stagnant and Truman repressed the urge to cough. They made their way through the passage until they reached the heavy, locked door that led to the antechamber of the nun's cell. Panting, father and son dropped Clarence onto the dank stone floor and Truman fed the key into the lock. The door creaked open and Truman approached the iron bars, lantern in hand. Behind him, he heard the sounds of shuffling boots and fabric on stone as Isaac dragged the prospector into the dank chamber.

"Is this the afflicted?" The voice that came from behind the bars sent a bitter chill racing down Truman's spine, like a January wind howling across the South Dakota prairie.

"It is. This is Clarence Conroy."

"Bring him to me."

Truman hesitated. "You told me that you could heal him. He's having violent tantrums. Some of the townsfolk want to lynch him because he's tried to attack other prospectors. He chased after one with a pickax. Sheriff Bullock's kept the vigilantes away so far, but this man's life ain't safe as long as he's like this."

The figure, shrouded in a long black tunic, stood statue-like behind the bars. A black veil covered not only the nun's hair but hid her face as well.

*"About damn time you got here,"* Bullock snarled at the approaching medicine man. *"She's fading fast."*

*"One of your deputies delayed me,"* Makohloka replied. *"I think he stopped my horse just because he saw my eagle feather headdress."*

*"We'll discuss that later. Do you have what the Sister requested?"*

*Makohloka pursed his lips and raised the object.*

*Truman, standing between the men, shuddered. "We'd better get moving, before it's too late."*

"Remove the cloth from his mouth and bring him to me," the voice repeated.

Truman made brief eye contact with Isaac and then the pair lifted the crazed man to his feet. Truman removed the makeshift gag and the skinny prospector immediately unleashed a torrent of angry sentences. Truman thought he recognized at least a couple of the words as Chinese. Clarence fixed a wide-eyed gaze on Mary Agnes and fell silent.

"Ask me what ails him," directed the voice from the cell.

"What ails—?"

"I'm talking to the boy."

Truman felt his face flush though he noticed his son's expression remained stoic.

"He can't speak. No tongue."

"Sorry to hear that. Truly, I am." The nun leaned toward Isaac, as if waiting for a response. When he didn't react, the nun's head swiveled back to Truman. "Is he deaf as well?"

"No. He just has a low tolerance for your bullshit."

The figure behind the bars surged forward. "Tell me how it happened! I love a good story!"

"Stop wasting time!" Truman demanded. "We're here to help Clarence. Do you know what ails him or not?"

"Of course. This fool has ingested a bowl of ghost soup."

"Ghost soup?"

"Chinese folklore contends that digging up and boiling the bones of the dead will yield a soup of highly medicinal properties. It doesn't."

"What *does* it do?" Truman asked.

"Opens a portal for angry spirits to return to this realm. Hui ta Wong is here with us. He's wearing the body of Clarence like a shabby old suit. His confusion is strong, but his anger and hatred are stronger. He tells me outlaws—*white* outlaws—raped his wife while he watched, then murdered them both for sport."

Truman glanced at the grizzled prospector as the voice continued.

"He'd like nothing more than to kill every white man he sees if given the chance."

"Can you remove the spirit? Take Mr. Wong out of Clarence and send his soul back where it belongs?"

"I can and I will. Bring him to me."

Truman didn't move. "Tell me what you intend to do first."

"There will be a kiss."

Truman felt his mouth fall open. "A kiss? Why?"

"I will pull the unwelcome spirit from him and save his life. The errant spirit will have no choice but to return to where it came from. Then all will be as it should."

Truman looked at Clarence. "Does the dead Chinaman inside Clarence know we're talking about sending him back?"

"Would he be standing here like a docile lamb waiting to be slaughtered if he knew? Of course not." The voice from the cell uttered a few Chinese words and the grubby little miner grinned.

"What did you say to him?" Truman asked.

"I offered to help him turn you inside-out and dance on your steaming entrails if he kissed me through the bars."

Truman instinctively reached for his Colt 45.

"Oh, unclench," the voice behind the bars chided. "Would you rather fight him every inch of the way in this little exorcism?"

Truman tried to find a calm that wasn't quite there. He caught Isaac's eye and they each took one of Clarence's arms and guided him to the bars.

*Truman Bonner, Sheriff Seth Bullock and the Lakota medicine man Makohloka, entered the nun's cell. Lantern light barely pushed back the darkness around them.*

*"Sister Mary?" Bullock said. "The Indian's here."*

*The woman opened her eyes and struggled into a sitting position. "Makohloka, do you have the talisman?"*

*The bronze-skinned man nodded. Sister Mary Agnes coughed and dark, wet flecks sprayed from her mouth.*

*Truman couldn't hold his tongue any longer. "Sister, you don't have to do this."*

*Sister Mary raised one hand in a feeble gesture for him to stop. Truman felt his mouth snap shut.*

*"Have you made your peace with your Savior, Sister?" Bullock asked. Truman thought he sounded embarrassed to be asking.*

*The nun nodded. "What happens next must be done. It is my choice. I ask only that you do it quickly and do it right."*

*The medicine man raised the arrow. The arrowhead resembled obsidian but Truman knew the truth. It moved very slowly, like a garden slug. Truman wished he had a Bible, though what good it would do he couldn't say.*

*Sister Mary eased back onto the blanket spread on the hard floor. Sheriff Bullock stepped back and placed his hand on the heavy cell door. Truman knew the plan. If this went to hell—literally or figuratively—they would sacrifice themselves in order to save countless others. Bullock would slam the door and lock the rest of them in.*

*Truman glanced once more at the arrowhead. He'd stood by when the old Chinaman, Shen Liu; the tall, bearded Preacher Smith; and Makohloka had clasped hands and each prayed in their native tongue. They'd cast a powerful spell. Yet already the arrowhead was losing its shape; the defensive shield they'd created was weakening.*

*Makohloka knelt and raised the arrow over his head in both hands. He slammed the tip through Sister Mary's ribs right above her heart. Her eyes flew open and blood spurted from her mouth. The medicine man leveraged his weight to snap the arrow's shaft, leaving the obsidian-like tip inside the nun's convulsing body.*

The nun lifted her veil, revealing papery, mummified skin. It reminded Truman of the dried outer layer of a yellow onion and his stomach clenched as the odor of dead, dried flesh reached his nostrils. Clarence—or Hui ta Wong—sensed the trap and howled with terror. Truman and Isaac braced themselves and held the smaller man against the iron.

Mary Agnes' skeletal face thrust between the bars and pressed against the raving man's lips. What looked to Truman like smoky gray syrup passed from the prospector's mouth and into the nun's. The afflicted

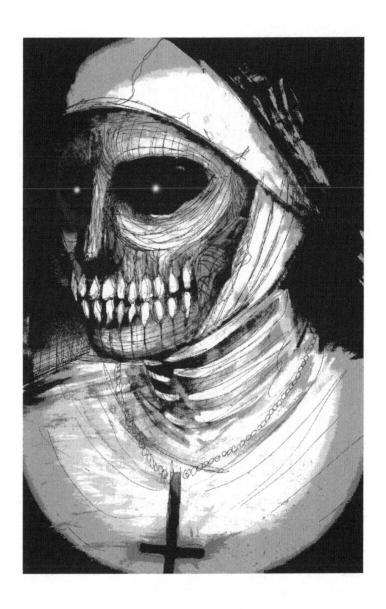

miner convulsed. His eyes rolled up in their sockets. The bulging whites contrasted with the hollow pockets of darkness in the skull of the nun. Truman felt the hair on the nape of his neck stand on end, as if hoping to uproot and relocate to calmer climes.

Then Mary Agnes fell to her knees and reached through the bars. It took a moment for Truman to realize the emaciated fingers had torn the front of the prospector's wool trousers. Before any of the men could react, the nun had taken Clarence's member in her mouth. Truman realized Isaac had loosened his hold on the old prospector's arm. He watched the proceedings with what looked like a mixture of curiosity and dismay.

Truman, feeling both amused and revolted himself, turned his gaze to Clarence. The grizzled prospector had stopped struggling. If anything, it looked as if he'd pressed himself harder against the bars. The skeletal head bobbed, the nun's habit obscuring most of the action. Truman felt his tenuous grasp of the situation rapidly dwindling. "That's enough!"

The nun paused and pulled away just enough to favor Truman with a yellow-toothed leer. "Hui ta Wong's soul proves to be rather stubborn. It doesn't want to leave. Do you want me to coax it out or don't you?"

Truman looked away. The nun resumed her ministrations. Truman moved to Isaac and led him to the corner of the antechamber. "I don't know how this is going to play out, but I apologize that you have to see this."

Clarence groaned with pleasure and Truman grimaced. The prospector erupted with a squeal of pain. Truman spun around. "*Teeeeth!*" Clarence cried. "She's scrapin' me wif' her teeth!" Truman realized he could understand the old man again. That meant the Chinaman's soul had left. He took a quick step forward and drew his sidearm.

Clarence had braced his grubby palms against the bars in an effort to pull away. Dark ruby rivulets of the prospector's blood dribbled down Sister Mary's bony chin. Truman realized that she was not going to release her captive unless he intervened.

*"Time to go," Truman urged the Lakota holy man. The pair hurried out of the cell and Bullock slammed the door behind them. He turned the key in the lock just as Sister Mary unleashed a scream so loud that it overwhelmed Truman's eardrums. Tears spilled from his eyes. Bullock staggered and covered his ears with his hands. Makohloka, looking as white as the others, mouthed an incantation Truman couldn't hear. Truman pinched his bandanna to his bleeding nose.*

*Sister Mary flew against the bars with brute force that shook dirt from the ceiling. Blood and spittle sprayed from her mouth and her fingernails raked at her chest.*

*"You goddamn goat fuckers," she croaked. "It burns like brimstone and sulfur pits in here!"*

"Let him go!" Truman thrust the barrel of the .45 through the bars and against the nun's skull. "Last chance!"

The nun ignored him. Truman pulled the trigger. The sound of thunder reverberated from the walls and deafened them. Dry bone fragments exploded into the air and against the cell wall. Truman's brain summoned up the image of goose feathers falling from a torn pillow.

The nun fell away and the prospector sagged into Isaac's arms. Truman silently applauded his son for stepping forward to catch the old fellow. Truman crouched and glanced at the prospector's member. It was bloody, but intact. A doctor would need to be summoned immediately. Truman looked up at Clarence's slack face and closed eyes. "Is he dead?" The words were out of Truman's mouth before he could stop them.

"He's cleansed," the voice in the cell snarled. The voice seemed quieter. Truman realized his ears still rang from the gunshot.

Truman held a hand beneath the limp man's nostrils. He felt the warmth of Clarence's ragged breathing and looked at Isaac. "Drag him out into the air, quick. Take him to a horse trough and splash water on his face. Then run and fetch a doctor."

Isaac cocked one eyebrow.

"Go ahead, I'll deal with her." Truman said.

The boy gritted his teeth and dragged the unconscious man along the stone floor. After they'd disappeared around the corner Truman turned back to the figure in the cell.

"The Chinaman's soul...you were able to retrieve it?"

"Oh my, yes. Two seconds after I kissed him."

Truman felt his cheeks grow hot. "But you said—"

"I lied! I just wanted to have a little fun."

The ash of indignation and the lava of rage welled up in Truman, but like Bear Butte, the nearby dead volcano, his fury had nowhere to go. He fumed with impotent rage. "Put the veil back down, for God's sake," he finally muttered.

"I do nothing for God's sake."

"Cover up, I said!"

"Does her face gall you that much?"

"It's *you* who galls me."

"How hurtful you are!" The nun yanked off her veil, then wrestled the habit up over her skull. The fabric rustled as it landed in the corner of the cell.

All that remained of Mary Agnes Gwyn now lay exposed. Truman winced. It wasn't her bleached white skeleton that galled him, it was the sinewy figure imprisoned in the dead nun's ribcage. Covered in reptilian scales and black as a mine-shaft at midnight, the unholy creature leered at him with glittering gold eyes.

"Desmod Kai," Truman whispered. "What an ugly little cuss you are."

The diminutive demon preened. "I'm stronger now."

"What are you getting at?" Truman asked. Icy fingertips of dread caressed his spine. "What did you do with the soul of the Chinaman?"

"I didn't send the spirit back. I ate it instead. Another mistake on your part and I'll have enough strength to break free."

"I'll never let that happen," Truman growled. Righteous assurance rose within him like a roaring prairie fire. "Despite what happened here, despite what *you* just did, Mary Agnes Gwyn was innocent and pure. She served her Lord in life. She made the ultimate sacrifice, letting you try to possess her body as she died. But the trap was sprung. Her spirit is at rest now, and her mortal coil still serves as an effective prison for you!"

The demon eyed Truman slyly. Its long talons made an abrasive sound as they scraped against the inside of her rib cage. The desire to return to his son came over the cowboy, sudden and strong.

"Her corpse is a cage, nothing more. And soon the cage will be *empty*," the demon said. The skeletal nun began a hideous, awkward dance, like a marionette pulled by invisible strings. From his ribcage prison, Desmod Kai gave Truman a jaunty little wave. "See you soon. And thanks for the meal."

Truman spun on his boot heel. He wanted to run but forced himself to walk. He would not give the little demon the satisfaction. Desmod Kai's laughter assaulted Truman's ears as he slammed the door and turned the key in the lock, leaving the creature in absolute darkness. Truman Bonner hurried through the winding passages, up the steps and out into the cool embrace of the night.

The ringing in Truman's ears faded with the passage of the night. The echoes of the demon's laughter, however, seemed to linger much longer.

# THERE'S NO WORD FOR IT

## *Adrian Ludens*

There's no word to describe the fear I suffer from. I've looked, believe me. I found lots of other phobias, but not one that describes my situation. There's pnigophobia, which is the fear of choking or being smothered. Seems like a valid concern. Phagophobia is almost the opposite; it's the fear of swallowing. Then there's the marvelous trio of acarophobia, entomophobia and insectophobia. Those are all the fear of insects. Despite my current predicament, none of these phobias have wound their icy, irrational fears around my psyche the way *this* has. Yet I still haven't found the official word for my most prominent fear.

The first insect I accidentally swallowed was most likely a mosquito. I was playing with my four-year-old nephew, Caleb, when it happened. I chased him on all fours as he squealed and scampered across our front lawn. I opened my mouth for what I hoped was a passable imitation of an angry bark and saw a small dot of black with cellophane wings darting through the air. The mosquito collided with the back of my throat and I swallowed automatically. I felt the prickle on the back of my throat where the mosquito had landed, but after a drink of cool water from the kitchen tap, the feeling went away. I thought no more about the incident until the second insect flew into my mouth later that same day.

It was after dinner, our visitors had gone, and I was puttering around outside. I started to yawn and caught a glimpse of green. Before I could react, I felt a tickle at the back of my throat.

I'd decided that it had been a green midge due to its coloring when I heard the low motor-like buzz of a bumblebee. It was joined by the electric drone of a horsefly. High pitched squealing in both ears announced the arrival of at least two more mosquitoes. I walked at first, and then jogged toward my front door, flailing my arms in an attempt at staving off the sudden swarm of insects. I unleashed a steam of expletives—and swallowed two bugs more before I made it inside.

That evening after the first wave of insects invaded my body, I almost took syrup of ipecac. Then I realized I'd rather let my stomach acid do its job than subject myself to the vomit-inducing wrath of that awful liquid. After all, I'd swallowed bugs, not poison. Looking back, I wish I had at least tried the ipecac, though I doubt it would have done any good.

Instead I did what any sane person would do; I tried to rationalize the situation. Failing at this, I fell back on the next best solution. I pretended that nothing out of the ordinary had happened.

That night I dreamed that a cell phone kept vibrating in my stomach.

I felt fine upon waking the next morning. I brushed my teeth, showered and dressed for work without remembering the bugs. I grabbed my briefcase, shoved the door open and trotted down the steps toward the driveway. What I saw stopped me in my tracks. Mayflies carpeted the hood and roof of my Impala. Suddenly uneasy, I turned on my heel and hurried back up the stairs.

Once safely within the confines of my home I pulled the curtain aside and gazed out the living room's picture window. Still in her pajamas, my wife, Samantha, padded into the room.

"I thought you'd left."

"Come look at this."

Samantha leaned to look where I pointed. "What?"

"Don't you see the mayflies all over my car?"

"What are you talking about, Will? I don't see anything."

I squinted. The white Impala looked gold thanks to the multitude of mayflies perched on it, their iridescent wings reflecting in the sun. I coughed without really needing to, stalling for time. "I think I might need to take some time off," I finally muttered.

Samantha's eyes twinkled. "Of course I see the mayflies! I'm just messing with you!"

I love my wife dearly but sometimes she seems to get a little too much enjoyment from making me feel foolish. Still, Samantha's beauty makes it easy for me to forgive her.

"Would you do me a huge favor?" I asked. "Would you go out there with a newspaper or something and chase them away for me?"

She put her hands on her hips and arched one eyebrow skeptically.

"Humor me, just this once," I begged.

Moments later, I watched from the window as Samantha approach my car holding yesterday's paper. She swung the makeshift weapon onto the hood and the mayflies took off *en masse,* creating a golden cloud that dissipated into the morning sky.

My wife grinned at me triumphantly. I hurried out to her. "I squashed a few and the rest flew off."

"Thanks honey." I kissed the top of her head. "This may sound crazy, but I was almost convinced that those things were deliberately waiting for me."

We laughed, and in that brief moment, a mayfly that had concealed itself beneath a crease in my wife's pajamas took to the air and flew into my mouth. The flutter of wings as it journeyed down my throat elicited a coughing fit within me. I pulled away from Samantha as the coughs wracked my frame. Then the feeling was gone, the newcomer apparently having joined its comrades.

During my commute, the wings of the crushed mayflies waved at me gaily from the hood of my Impala, proud martyrs in the war against my sanity.

Insects targeted me for the next three days. They flew—and sometimes crawled—into my mouth at every opportunity. I saw a few miller moths, although they easily could have been meal moths. A honey bee hovered around my head for several minutes before giving up. A bumblebee tried to fly into my mouth but I slapped it aside at the last second. It stung the back of my hand instead. I damn near choked to death when that gladiator katydid crawled down my throat.

I broke down and tried the syrup of ipecac. It made me vomit, but to my great dismay no dead insects appeared in the toilet bowl.

Thursday afternoon, on my way home from work, I stopped at Bloom Hardware and scooped up an armload of insect repellents. I waddled up and down the aisles, cradling my brood of aerosol cans, spray bottles and baited traps. As an afterthought, I selected a package of those white filter masks you sometimes see allergy-prone people wear when they're out mowing.

"Bug problems?" the cashier asked as I unloaded my selections down on the counter.

I started to reply and right at that moment a ladybug sped through the air and straight down my gullet. I felt tears of frustration well up, and I glowered at the clerk.

"What the hell is a ladybug doing in a hardware store anyway? Don't you people spray against that kind of thing?"

Samantha smiled at the array of insect repellents I had purchased. She waited patiently as I grimly squirted the windowsills and around our doors, both inside and out. When my hand ached from pumping the spray handle, I simply switched to the other hand. I sprayed our hedges, the exteriors of our vehicles, the mailbox, and everything else I could think of. I even dragged the wooden ladder from the garage and sprayed around all the exteriors of the windows on the second floor. I positioned poisoned bait traps in every corner and hung flypaper from the ceiling of each room. After three hours I staggered into the bedroom. I felt dizzy from the effects of the chemicals and there was a buzzing in my ears.

Samantha, now in her pajamas, wordlessly laid out a bath towel and turned on the shower for me. She wasn't smiling any more.

I cleaned up, toweled off and pulled on my pajamas. I couldn't get the insects out of my mind. Haunted by a vision of a caravan of bugs marching across my pillow and into my mouth while I slept, I returned to the hardware store bag on the kitchen counter. I pulled on one of the white filter masks and fitted it over my mouth and nose. Samantha looked alarmed as I crawled under the covers beside her.

"Will," she entreated. "I love you, but don't you think you're taking this a little too far?"

"Something is making insects want to fly in through my mouth to my stomach," I declared. "That's not natural, damn it! Until I find out what's going on, the mask stays on."

"Look, I'm sorry this is happening to you."

"I'll check in the phone book tomorrow morning," I assured her as I clicked off the lamp. "A specialist will know what to do."

Samantha rolled toward me and pecked my cheek above the white mask.

"Good night, sleep tight, don't let the bed bugs bite," she said and giggled uncertainly. Then she rolled away from me. I didn't try to comfort or reassure her. I'd become preoccupied with the buzzing again. I could still hear it, but it wasn't in my ears like I had first thought. The buzzing came from my stomach.

The next morning, I sat on the edge of the bathtub and evacuated my bowels. It took longer than I'd expected to overcome the urge to sit on the toilet. At last

I was able to break from of my deeply ingrained directive. After wiping, I pulled on a pair of Samantha's dishwashing gloves and began to systematically and carefully examine my feces.

"What are you doing, Will?"

I jumped at the sound of my wife's voice. "I am conducting an examination of my excrement." Part of me realized how ridiculous I must have sounded. You can't polish a turd, after all. "I'm doing this in hopes of finding wings, legs or some other evidence that the insects are dying and being naturally expelled."

Still kneeling, my arms hanging limply over the edge of the tub, I stole a glance over my shoulder. Samantha's face had paled. She didn't say a word. Instead, she took a careful step back, turned on her heel and hurried down the hallway. I heard the front door open and close. I held my breath until I heard the distant sound of her car starting. I listened as she drove away. I wondered when she'd be back.

Even more troubling, I found no insect presence in my feces.

Although I went to work on Friday, I accomplished little in my preoccupied state. I asked my supervisor for the next week off, citing health issues. I then spent the weekend dousing the house with more insect repellent. Each morning I examined my bowel movements but was disappointed by the results.

Samantha phoned me Sunday evening to say that although she was worried about me she would be staying with friends until I had resolved my issues. That's what she called them: *issues*, not problems. I assured her that I had made seeing a doctor my top priority.

When Monday arrived, the first ear, nose and throat specialist I contacted refused to take me seriously. It was the same with the second one I called, and with the third. The general practitioner at Bloom Memorial Hospital who fit me in on short notice refused to examine me once he had heard my complaint. Instead he gave me the business card of a psychologist who practiced nearby. Out of spite, I slipped a stethoscope into my jacket after the jackass had left the room and shredded the business card on my way out.

At home, I sat in my leather recliner and used the purloined instrument to listen to the cacophony of buzzing, chirping and droning coming from inside my distended stomach.

If doctors weren't going to hear me out long enough to actually help me, I'd have to find another way. I'd have to arrange for an "accidental" discovery of the insects within me. I ruminated on the matter while attempting to drown my unwelcome guests in scotch.

After a couple of hours and double that many scotches I felt I had concocted a foolproof idea: gastric bypass surgery. During the procedure the doctor would surely see that something was amiss.

I lay back in my recliner, feeling very self-satisfied. Even though I had tossed the stethoscope aside, I could still hear the bugs. In fact, it was the interior chirping of crickets that eventually lulled me to sleep.

"I'm sorry sir, but based on the information you have provided, you simply are not a candidate for gastric bypass surgery." The woman from Bloom Memorial sounded bored.

"You don't understand." I clutched the receiver in one hand and rubbed my churning stomach with the other. "I *need* this!"

"I'm sorry. You simply don't weigh enough to—"

"Damn it, listen to me! I need someone to take a look at my stomach!"

"Sir, if you'll calm down, I will explain your options to you." Now the woman sounded both bored and annoyed simultaneously.

"I'm calm," I lied.

"I would advise you to call your health insurance company. You have to understand that this would fall into the category of elective surgery. Most likely your insurance company will not cover the procedure, but you should contact them first for possible pre-approval. They might let you apply the cost of the procedure toward your deductible," the woman prattled.

My hands shook. I felt sick. The scotch was long gone and I'd moved on to whiskey. Since Samantha was not in the house, I didn't bother using a glass. I swallowed my mounting panic and washed it down with a swig from the bottle. I fidgeted in my chair as the woman went on.

"Of course, whether or not we happen to be in-network providers with your particular insurance company will affect how much help you'd be getting from them. Depending on the plan you have, some insurance companies might require you to undergo a complete physical before allowing you to schedule elective surgery. Then there's the possibility that—"

Finally giving voice to my mounting revulsion, I shrieked and threw the phone across the room. An emergency room visit had taken two years of phone calls to my insurance company before it got paid. Always there were the loopholes, the missing paperwork, the additional information required. I couldn't face all that again.

Bugs were hell-bent on climbing into my mouth. I didn't need my insurance company trying to climb up my ass. Having a choice between "A" and "B" was no choice at all. There had to be an easier way.

I drained the contents of the bottle and mentally formulated my plan for deliverance. Having resolved myself on this alternate plan of action, I rose and headed for the kitchen. A lone fly pattering against the window pane turned its attention toward me as I entered. I grabbed my car keys off the counter and opened my mouth for the approaching fly. Why not one more for the road?

I careened toward Bloom Hardware, madly singing "I Know an Old Lady Who Swallowed a Fly." I was halfway through my seventh rendition, gleefully bellowing "perhaps she'll diiiiiieeeee!" when I spun the wheel and guided the Impala into a handicapped spot near the store's entrance.

I left the car door hanging open and trotted into the store's interior. My stomach felt bloated, itchy, and unsettled. I was painfully conscious of every move the bugs were making inside me and I muttered under my breath, entreating them to keep still. It had begun to feel like an interior rash. I scanned the signs hanging above the aisles until I located the one I wanted: Gardening.

"Can I help you find anything today, sir?" asked the green-vested teenager who'd materialized beside me.

"I would like to obtain the strongest insecticide you have on hand. Not the stuff meant for household purposes, but something a farmer or a professional greenhouse would use."

"Sure. We keep that in the back."

"Would you please go get it and meet me back here as soon as you can?"

He nodded and we parted ways. The kid made it back in four minutes, but I was back in two. His eyebrows furrowed when he saw what I had acquired.

"Is that the strongest stuff you've got?" I lifted my chin toward the large black aerosol can he carried.

"Yes sir. Guaranteed to kill all types of insects on contact."

"I want you to pop the lid off that can and get ready to spray it. Understand?"

The kid had paled. His eyes seemed to be glued to the garden shears I held. "I should call my manager."

"Aim right here," I pointed at my midriff. "Get ready to spray..."

Envisioning a dishonored Samurai warrior, I lifted the shears over my head, and then swung down as hard as I could. There was a wet snap as the blades punctured the lining of my stomach. Before the pain kicked in full force, I pulled the wet blades back out, turned them at an angle in my right hand and sliced my stomach wide open.

"Now!" I bellowed.

Instead of insecticide, the kid sprayed his half-digested lunch out onto the tiled floor. For my part, I sprayed profuse amounts of dark red blood, stomach bile and enough harbored insects to impress even Noah.

I became dimly aware of the kid shouting. I think he was trying to yell for an ambulance, but his words came out all garbled. Maybe I should have let him get his manager after all.

I glanced up at the army of insects that crawled, skittered, and hovered in the aisle around and above me. It was as if the multitude were considering the situation. I struggled toward the insecticide sprayer lying in the aisle where the kid had dropped it. I brandished the spray and the insects dissipated in all directions. They *finally* realized they were not welcome.

The sharp pain in my stomach was already fading, and a warm, muzzy feeling began to envelop me. I sank completely to the sticky tile, my head swimming. Darkness rapidly narrowed my field of vision.

I felt like laughing. I had won. I was free. Best of all, I didn't have to deal with my insurance company. The endless cycle of letters and phone calls; the rules, regulations, exclusions and the dreaded rejected claims.

What would one call a pronounced fear of, and aversion to, dealing with health insurance companies? From what I have researched, there's no word for it.

# THE EXCITEMENT NEVER ENDS

## *Adrian Ludens*

For a moment pain inundates my entire being.

I open my eyes and take a deep breath. I must have dozed off on one of the amusement park benches. Where'd he go? Ah, there he is. I stand up to follow him and a woman pushing a squalling child in a stroller grimaces as I cross her path though she doesn't seem to see me—and I only have eyes for the boy.

He has skin of porcelain. A young Michelangelo's David, he is. I admire him from afar as he and his mousy little female friend—I judge them too young to be boyfriend and girlfriend—ride the Tilt-A-Whirl, one of many rides and attractions at Happyland. Here, according to the slogan on their sign of welcome, "Where the Excitement Never Ends!" Soon I will approach the boy. I want to touch that perfect skin.

Lady Luck just blew me a kiss! The boy departs the ride in a hurry, leaving the girl behind. He runs, skin white as milk, toward the cinderblock restrooms. I follow him in.

His skin is not porcelain after all. I feel lied to, foolish. He was only sick! He vomited his corn dog, lime slushy, and caramel corn (I did a cursory inventory, so what?) into a toilet bowl that isn't porcelain either. In his hurry, he failed to latch the door to the stall. I did it for him on my way in. Now his face is peaked, with purple half-moons under his eyes. Not what I'd hoped for at all. I've lost interest. I decide to leave before the boy ruins everything. He panics.

But now I don't know what's happening. Honest. I'd decided to leave. The boy isn't in any danger, but does he think to ask? No. He assumes the worst. He opens his mouth as if to scream so I punch him in the throat, just to buy myself some time. I think maybe he'll calm down but he clutches his chest instead. He flops around on the dank concrete like a fish out of water. I feel sorry for fish. People don't think they can feel pain or fear, but I think they do. The boy, he dies before I can do anything to help him. Horrible business.

I undress him, just to see his skin, and then I prop the boy on the toilet, and lean him back so he doesn't fall. I don't feel like admiring his skin now. Lady Luck has had no involvement in my day after all. I peek over the stall door. All clear. I drop to the floor and scuttle crab-like out of the stall, leaving it locked behind me. That should buy me another minute or two to put some space between us. Out the exit, easy peasy.

Goddamn it. The girl. She looks right at me. Looks me right in the eye as I walk past. Did she see me follow her friend inside the bathrooms? She's going to cause trouble, I can tell. Move. Mingle. Disappear. Don't look back. Don't. Okay, just once. Shit. A janitor. Seriously? I didn't even know Happyland employed them. He's going in. Screw this—I'm gone.

What in hell? Do I have gum on the soles of my shoes or has the hot sun melted the asphalt beneath me? It seems to take forever before I feel safe. I look back find the girl and keep my eye on her; walking in big concentric circles around her position. She's become my world. I orbit around her like the moon. I see that security has arrived. Skinny little guy in a golf cart. He joins the girl and the janitor. I need to go. Get gone. Leave the premises. Yet I stay. I need to make sure the girl doesn't tell them about me.

The janitor and security guard enter the bathroom. The moment lengthens, becomes interminable. The odors of fried foods and motor oil intermingle. Shrieks of laughter stab the muggy summer air. Garish colors and tinny music prevail. Then the pair reemerges. The security guy is speaking into a walkie talkie. The janitor slumps against the cinder block wall. And the girl turns and begins to run. Her face betrays a mixture of sorrow and denial. Maybe she was his girlfriend after all.

I realize she's heading for the main gate to the park. For her, and everyone inside Happyland, it's the exit. Witness for the prosecution, please exit stage left. I can't let her. I'm closer than she is. I join the race already in first place. I merge through the throng, edging ever closer to my surrogate quarry, my prey by proxy. Her skin is spattered with freckles and moles. I'm appalled, but I swallow my revulsion mere feet from the gate and reach out my hands. Normally she'd be of no interest to me, but this is strictly damage control.

The girl's eyes widen with terror and recognition and she tries to duck out of my grasp. No dice honey. I scoop her up. She tries to scream but I clamp one hand over the lower half of her face. "Now, Nancy, don't make such a fuss." I say, loud enough for others to hear. "We've had a nice time at the amusement park but it's time to go home. Now's not the time for a tantrum, young miss." I walk toward the gate. She flails in my grasp. "Don't be a brat!"

I say. No one stops us. No one lifts a finger, or even looks twice.

I just want to talk to her, to explain. She'll see I have an honest face. She'll understand that what happened was an accident. She has to.

The parking lot is another world. It's not nearly as crowded and the rules are different. At first I stop short, just trying to figure out what the hell I'm looking at. There's a man with a gun. Not a handgun, or a hunting rifle, but a machine gun. A semi-automatic weapon hangs slung over his back. I slow, not wanting to attract the lunatic's attention. In my confusion, I step off the curb. I stagger and my precious cargo and I thump into a dusty hybrid SUV. My hand falls away from her mouth. It's only for a second, but it's too much time.

"HELLLLP!" The girl screams. The man with the weapon spins around. I try to smile, but it feels more like a maniacal leer. "My kid," I say. "Spoiled. She's trying to make a scene."

The man points his gun at me. "Drop the girl and back away, perv-o." I look past the long black weapon, which reminds me of a scorpion's poised tail, and take a look at his t-shirt. On it, a man with a long white goatee stands before a wooden cross. He's wearing a crown of thorns and star-spangled jacket and spats. He's carrying a blazing assault rifle in each holy (and holey) hand. I realize this is a shoot-first-and-ask-questions-later kind of guy. There'll be no reasoning with him.

I panic. I grab the girl's wrists and spin around, draping her over my shoulders like a bulletproof cape. I execute the ingenious maneuver with too much gusto and I hear one of her shoulders dislocate as I turn to run. I'm trying to cover a king size bed with a twin size blanket and it just won't work. The girl's agonized screams pierce my eardrum with every shambling step I take. At least I've temporarily neutralized the gunman.

Damn it, I'm (we're) back at the gate. Welcome to Happyland, The Excitement Never Ends! Kiss my ass already, I think. Then I draw up short. The barrel of the handgun pressed into my left nostril becomes my entire world. I forget about everything else because I forgot about the security guard. His finger is white on the trigger. I try to talk him out of it. "You can't—"

But he does. For a moment pain inundates my entire being.

I open my eyes and take a deep breath. I must have dozed off on one of the amusement park benches. Where'd he go? Ah, there he is. I stand, and this time a balding man in a Nebraska t-shirt frowns and hunches his shoulders as I pass him by.

The boy still has skin of porcelain. A young Michelangelo's David, he is. Soon I will approach the boy but for the moment I admire him from afar. He and his mousy little female friend—I judge them too young to be boyfriend and girlfriend—ride the Tilt-A-Whirl, one of many rides and attractions at Happyland. Here, according to the slogan on their sign of welcome, "Where the Excitement Never Ends!"

# A MISADVENTURE TO CALL YOUR OWN

## *Adrian Ludens*

"You'll pay dearly for what happened every day for the rest of your miserable life!"

It's not a proclamation one wants to hear first thing in the morning. You open your eyes to the dim interior of your bedroom and search for the voice's source. Perhaps you'd only heard the interior dialogue of a vivid dream.

"You'll pay financially, emotionally and physically," the strident voice continues. "I'll bleed you dry, until you're left with nothing but worry and suffering."

Apparently something is amiss, but whatever you may have done, this sounds like overkill. You sit up amidst a tangled sheet and gaze blearily at the speaker. As your eyes adjust to the light, you see a short slender figure, their arms crossed in judgment. The speaker's hair is tousled to the point of disarray. The speaker is naked, and has addressed you from the foot of the bed.

Your bed. The bed you share with your One True Love. You squint again.

Who is this?

*If you realize you are simply role-playing with your One True Love, turn to page 3.*
*If you recognize that the speaker is an elderly neighbor who must be having one of their 'bad spells', turn to page 4.*

*If you're too hung-over to remember what happened last night, take two aspirin and turn to page 5.*

Feeling hung over and still quite confused as to what events transpired over the past few hours, you raise your hands in a pleading gesture. You need time to think.

*Who is this person? How did they get here?*

The figure pads around the bed and leans down so the two of you are eye to eye. The sour scent of mixed drinks wafts around your head and a wave of nausea threatens to drown your calm. *Uh-oh.* Now you recognize the face; and it's from a distant past you'd rather not revisit.

"You won't be able to explain this when your significant other returns from that business trip," your guest—who has most certainly overstayed their welcome— hisses in your ear. "There's no way out!"

You open your mouth to respond, but your tongue is a shriveled and lifeless mummy curled in the corner of your mouth. You didn't have a witty retort ready anyway.

"Apparently you thought I wasn't good enough for you so you moved on." Your accuser trembles with rage; or possibly excitement. "But I tracked you down at the bar last night; got you to take me home. After what we did—after what *you* did—you belong to *me* now! I pull the strings now, Puppet. Bow down to your new Master."

A sliver of drool dives gracefully from your guest's bottom lip and disappears into the folds of your rumpled sheet. You decide they're trembling from excitement.

"What will you do now?" Your new Master inquires.

*If you decide to call your One True Love immediately to confess everything, turn to page 8.*
*If you just remembered you've been concealing an ice pick under the pillow all along, turn to page 10.*
*If you realize all this talk has made you hungry, turn to page 12.*

"I need to get some food in my stomach," you announce as you push aside the sheet and stand beside your guest. "Let's go up to the kitchen and discuss this like rational adults."

Feeling a pair of angry eyes burning into your bare back, you shuffle up the stairs feigning a calm that isn't quite there. In the kitchen, you grab lunch meat, processed cheese slices and mayo from the refrigerator.

You can hear soft footsteps behind you. A board creaks but you don't look. You need to come up with a plan. You decide a steak knife might level the playing field, so you pull open the silverware drawer. Your hand freezes in midair. All the knives are gone.

Your guest snickers behind you. "Do you think I'm that stupid? I hid the knives before coming downstairs to confront you. What do you think about that?"

*If you want to grab a fork and try to do the job anyway, scream "Fork you!" and turn to page 14.*
*If you want to grab a cool beverage and see what's on television, turn to channel 16.*
*If you want to grab your accuser and give them a kiss to trick them into dropping their guard, turn to page 17.*

You grin and cross the kitchen. You reach out with both hands but this move is one your guest clearly does not welcome.

"Back off!" your former lover turned one-night stand turned blackmailer warns, and you notice they don't look too confident all of a sudden. Instead of stopping you lunge in for a claustrophobic I-could-never-stay-mad-at-you hug.

"Let me go!" your guest complains and presses both palms against your shoulders in an effort to leverage their body free.

You unclasp your hands and your blackmailer staggers backward. Their arms flail and your guest tumbles ass over teakettle down your stairs.

Gazing down at the body sprawled at the bottom of the stairwell you realize immediately that your unwelcome guest is dead. You've seen enough broken necks in movies to draw your own conclusion: this looks completely phony, so it *must* be real.

You slump against the cool counter and consider your next move.

*If you want to dispose of the body right away, turn to page 20.*

*If you want to grab that cool beverage and finally see what's on television, turn to channel 16 already.*

*If you just noticed that there's a new message on your answering machine and you haven't listened to it yet, turn to page 21.*

Gazing across the room you notice the red light on your answering machine staring at you like an accusing eye. You wonder who called. You never heard the phone ring, so perhaps the call came last night when you were otherwise indisposed. Knowing you'll never be able to focus on the problem at hand until you've heard the message, you approach the phone. You reach out a shaky finger and pause. Instead of a miniature devil and angel verbally sparring on your shoulders, fear of discovery battles obsessive compulsion.

Is checking your messages really a priority right now? Would any rational, sane person be distracted by this? The answer is no. But still, you are curious about who called...

*If you think the message is from a bill collector, press delete and turn to page 22.*

*If you think the message is from a bill collector, but you plan to cite a segment you saw on the news about fraudulent bill collectors as an excuse not to pay, slyly turn to page 23.*

*If you think the message might be worth hearing, because it may turn out to have some plot-convenient bearing on your present situation, press play and turn to page 24.*

You press the playback button and hear your mother's voice:

"Hello dear. I'm afraid I have some sad news. Your Uncle Marlin passed away two days ago."

This isn't sad news. Hearing of the demise of Uncle "Bad Touch" brings a sneer to your lips.

"I should have called you sooner but I've been so busy up here at his farmhouse putting things in order. Services will be held at Trailside Church the day after tomorrow at noon. I know it's a two-hour drive up, but I'd appreciate it if you'd attend."

You wonder if he died of natural causes or if one of your cousins paid an unannounced visit to his ramshackle farm for some payback. You chew on your bottom lip and mull the situation over.

Uncle Marlin lived on a farm seven miles north of the tiny community of Trailside. The church where the funeral will take place is on the outer edge of a town of fewer than one thousand people. You decide this scenario has some definite possibilities.

*If you decide to call the funeral parlor to ask about "two for one pricing" turn to page 26.*
*If you decide your uncle's farm would be the perfect place to dispose of the body, turn to page 27.*
*If you decide your uncle's funeral would provide the perfect opportunity to dispose of the body instead, turn to page 28.*

You decide to attend the funeral and to bring a guest. The situation could provide a unique opportunity for the disposal of the body in your basement.

After two glasses of blood lite—your sobriquet for red wine—to fortify your faltering nerve, you descend the stairs.

The first order of business is to grab several hand towels from the bathroom cupboard to wipe up; there's no blood, but the loosened bowels and voided bladder make for a more voluminous mess than a few squares of toilet tissue can handle.

This accomplished, the soiled towels go straight into the washing machine and you scrub your hands for several minutes longer than is necessary.

Next you decide to wrap the body in a spare bed sheet. You choose one covered with tiny fabric pills that make it uncomfortable to sleep on. You made this purchase long before you learned about thread count or fabric quality and decide it also deserves to be buried in the ground.

You also backtrack to your bedroom to gather your guest's clothing and belongings. Rather than try to dress the body you tuck the articles of clothing around limbs so they'll stay in place. You straighten and survey your work.

*If you decide you're too attached to that old sheet to part with it after all, turn to page 31.*
*If you remember reading somewhere that lime helps speed decomposition, turn to page 32.*
*If you can't shake the urge to wash your hands again, turn to page 33.*

You remember reading somewhere that lime helps speed decomposition, so you trudge back upstairs to check your fridge for the little green fruit. You come up empty, which should be no surprise since you can't even remember the last time you've used lime in a drink. Besides, slicing up a lime doesn't quite seem right. Isn't the lime supposed to be in powder form?

Feeling perplexed, you scan the kitchen seeking inspiration. Your eyes fall on the spice rack. *Lemon pepper! Not perfect, but it will do,* you decide.

You take the stairs two at a time back down and sprinkle liberal amounts of your find on the body. Inspiration strikes again and you retrieve spring-scented carpet powder ("eliminates pet and other offensive odors!") and shower your guest with that as well.

Satisfied at last, you wrap the body up in the sheet and tie off both ends with their shoelaces.

Exhausted by your exertions, you tumble into bed for some much-needed rest.

*If your sleep is plagued by nightmares of masked Mexican wrestlers pulling your teeth out with pliers (and whose isn't?) turn to page 35.*
*If sleep never comes because the moment you lie down the phone won't stop ringing, get back up and turn to page 36.*
*If you sleep well but awaken to the ominous tolling of a grandfather clock announcing the witching hour, turn to page 37.*

Your heirloom grandfather clock pulls you from the irresponsibility of sleep and chimes twelve times. This, you decide, is the perfect time to move your visitor from the stairwell to the trunk of your car.

You dress quickly, and haul your cargo by the ankles up the stairs. You reach the kitchen and let their legs drop. Panting, you shuffle out your front door for a little advance recon. The street is empty. The houses are dark.

Even the moon cooperates by discretely ducking behind a rolling cloud bank.

Staggering under the weight of your burden, you reach the open trunk and deposit the body inside.

Another glass of wine and it's off to bed to lie awake, anxiously waiting for morning. You think of your One True Love away on business and the unsavory business you must attend to before their return. You remember your brief fling—many years ago—with the deceased. You think about your favorite movie, the best concert you ever attended and the last good book you've read. All the while the sun crawls around the earth. You force yourself to wait until just after seven a.m. to dress and leave the house.

The drive north out of the city is a dull one but soon you are daydreaming about what you would do with the power of invisibility.

You are so absorbed in your imaginary escapades that you don't see the police cruiser easing up behind your car until the officer turns on his flashers and gives your eardrums a short burst of siren. The siren's song, true to legend, is one that conjures up fear but is extremely difficult to ignore.

*If you were speeding, slow down, use your turn signal and ease onto the shoulder located on page 38.*

*If you were not speeding but realize your tags are expired, turn to page 39.*

*If you thought you'd get through a dead-body-in-the-trunk adventure without getting pulled over by an ornery rural cop, turn to page 40.*

A big-bellied sheriff's deputy with a Smokey the Bear hat tipped back on his bullet head ambles toward your car. Even with his eyes hidden behind out-of-date mirrored sunglasses, you can see the smug satisfaction on his face.

His unsnaps the holster strap on his sidearm and rests his palm on the butt of his gun. With his other palm he scratches his butt. You repress a smile.

"Well, well," the cop begins. "Somebody from the city is driving through my stretch of country in an awful hurry."

You do your best to appear both sheepish and contrite and wait for him to continue.

"You were speeding, your tags are expired and for all I know, you've got a dead body in the trunk."

At first all the blood drains from your face, then it catapults back up and brands your cheeks with guilt.

You realize the officer is waiting for you to respond.

*If you've stopped near the bridge that stretches over Owl Creek and feel inspired to try to make a harrowing and adventurous dash for freedom, turn to page 42.*

*If you try to intimidate the officer by cranking up some vintage gangsta rap on your stereo, turn the volume up to 43.*

*If you nod sheepishly and admit, "Two out of three officer; you got me" hold your breath and turn to page 45.*

You finally decide to nod sheepishly and admit, "Two out of three officer; you got me."

Despite an inexplicable sense of *déjà vu*, you feel cautiously optimistic. Even if the officer writes you a ticket for either, or both, infractions, chances are against him asking to look in the trunk.

Without warning a shrill howl raises the hair on your neck and goose bumps do the wave up and down your arms.

The deputy has tilted his head back to let loose a second barbaric yawp. Then he grins. "Lone Wolf sniffs out another perpetrator," he exclaims and juts his chin out proudly.

You glance at the nameplate just below his badge and notice his name is Moranus but you decide it prudent to let him have his moment.

Two citations later you drive away, careful to stay five miles under the posted limit. Your forehead is drenched with sweat and your mouth is dry as alkali, but the secret in your trunk remains undiscovered. "Two out of three ain't bad," you mumble.

You are still thanking your lucky stars ten miles down the road when your vision blurs and a sharp pain hits you.

*If the pain is in your right temple, turn to page 48.*
*If the pain is in your left arm, turn to page 49.*
*If the pain is in the right lower quadrant of your belly, just above your hip bone, try to locate the appendix.*

You hit the brakes and kick up a spray of gravel and dust as you guide your car onto the shoulder of the road.

Once the car's forward momentum has stopped, you grimace and stretch your arms. Alternately massaging each forearm, you concentrate on relaxing. A deep inhalation, count to ten and exhale. You do this several times, flexing your fingers and running them through your hair. Not a heart attack; just muscle cramps from gripping the steering wheel too tightly.

You tell yourself to relax. Based on the scenery, you think the Trailside Church should only be a few more miles ahead. Your uncle's farm is seven miles farther north of Trailside.

It's time to make another decision.

*If you decide to turn back and risk getting pulled over again as you head for home, turn to page 51.*
*If you decide to pass the church and continue on to your uncle's farm, turn to page 52.*
*If you decide to stop at the church to make sure that creep is really dead, turn to page 53.*

The Trailside Church is an unassuming little building. It has seen a few weddings, more than its fair share of funerals and even a baptism or two. Finding the parking lot full, you double park beside the waiting hearse and jog up the stone stairs.

You ease the door open and slide into the narthex. As your eyes adjust to the dim interior you realize you are not alone.

Nearby is the cheapest casket the family could apparently find and nestled inside is your late Uncle Marlin. You feel your lips press in a tight line and clench your hands until your nails dig into your palms. You wish you could inflict some suffering or indignity upon him.

You step forward and look through the narrow window into the sanctuary, which your mother insisted upon calling the nave because she believed it made her sound more cultured. The figures in the rows make a sea of black, dotted with whitecaps of gray, white, blue and bald. A sleepy looking preacher reads predictable passages from a tattered Bible at a wooden podium near the altar.

You return to the casket and look at your uncle again. Perhaps there is some extra room...

"Hey there," a voice you don't recognize demands. "Who are you?"

*If you explain that you are a member of the clergy administering "De Facto Last Rites of Duplication" turn to page 54.*
*If you explain that you are the mortician's assistant and that you are "Just topping off fluids" turn to page 55.*
*If you retort "I could ask you the same question!" turn to page 56.*

Failing to come up with anything more creative, you curtly reply, "I could ask you the same question!"

The narthex is now filled with the odor of raw rhubarb mixed with cat pee and you narrow your eyes at the young man who has spoken. You don't recognize him as a relation so you decide he must live here in Trailside and is here with his folks, probably against his will. It shouldn't be hard to get rid of him.

"Did you sneak out for a couple hits?" you ask, feigning disapproval. The teen averts his bloodshot eyes and you cross your arms. He hurries past you into the sanctuary and slides into an empty spot next to an oblivious parental unit in a pew near the back.

You notice everyone inside has bowed their heads either in prayer or weariness, so you *carpe diem* and hurry back to your car. A quick scan of the parking lot shows that the coast is clear for the moment; perhaps everyone in town is inside the church with their backs collectively turned away from you.

You pop the trunk, hoist the body over your shoulder and hustle up the stairs. Adrenaline surges through your limbs as you slip back inside and triumphantly dump your cargo into the casket on top of your uncle.

You tip the lid down but it won't close. Lifting the lid back up you realize that you'll need to readjust the casket's contents.

The congregation of mourners and small-town gawkers has risen in their pews to mumble a hymn. You yank the body back out and replace it so that it lays face down with the head resting between your uncle's feet. Panting, you glance over your shoulder and find the coast is still clear. Everyone is still in the nave and you're still craving knavery.

*If you take a moment to shave your uncle's out-of-control eyebrows, go to page 60.*
*If you take a moment to say a few choice parting words to the deceased (plural), go to page 61.*
*If you flip them both the bird, close the lid and make a run for it, turn to page 62.*

Your uncle's "old geezer" brows bristle like defensive caterpillars. Seeing this as the perfect opportunity for some admittedly petty but worthwhile revenge you fumble around in your pockets for your ring of keys. On the key ring is also a tiny utility knife. You select it, cupping your keys in your hand and opening the knife's blade.

"You two deserve each other," you mutter and extend the middle finger of your free hand at the new roommates. Then you lean in and scrape the blade against your uncle's skin, shaving off one eyebrow in three strokes. Just as you are about to move on to the other side, a surge in the volume of singing warns you that the sanctuary door has been opened.

You drop the lid to the casket as quick as you can and turn to look behind you.

A dour-faced man strides forward. He carries a battered leather case and wears a large enamel name tag that reads:

*Jolley Brothers Funeral Services*
*Bryan Bruce, Director*

"Excuse me; what are you doing with the deceased?"

This time you're prepared. In fact, you have so many excuses ready you'll need to narrow it down first.

*If you want to reveal that your uncle had expressed his wish for a closed-casket ceremony and you are simply honoring the dear old saint's wishes, solemnly turn to page 64.*

*If you want accuse the mortician of shoddy workmanship and explain that you closed the casket lid out of necessity, haughtily turn to page 65.*

*If you want to reveal that you just drove a wooden stake through his black and centuries-old heart, turn to page 67.*

"I noticed that one of my uncle's eyelids has collapsed," you explain to the man in hushed tones. You lead him away from the casket before continuing. "I closed the lid so that none of my uncle's loved ones would notice and become upset."

Mr. Bruce shakes his head and mutters, "We can certainly fix—"

You have to stop that train of thought before it leaves the station so you plunge with the only dagger at your disposal. "I'd hate to think what would happen if the relatives got together and demanded a refund."

The funeral director's mouth snaps shut as if wired closed and filled with cotton. Time to give the dagger a delicate twist to make sure the subject dies.

"Think of the small-town scandal!" you murmur. "I'm sure you and I agree it would be best to leave well enough alone."

Mr. Bruce nods like it's the best idea he's heard in decades. He instructs the pallbearers, who have just arrived from the sanctuary to carry the casket out to the hearse. The six of them grunt and heft their special cargo to the waiting car. Mr. Bruce slides in behind the wheel and leads the procession of mourners across the gravel road and into the gates of the adjacent Trailside Cemetery.

A group of clucking hens (your aunts) files past you. Your mother is among them and she smiles wanly as she passes. You amble along with the stragglers but once you reach the open grave you find yourself pushing to the front of the group.

The pallbearers heft the casket out of the hearse and place it on the faded straps of the lowering device. The dithering preacher says a few more words about ashes and dust bunnies, and you wonder how much of this he could have said while still inside the church. You glance around and see many closed eyes and vacant stares. *Why is this taking so long?*

At last the casket is lowered into the hole. A few of your cousins don't look upset in the least. Normally you'd be able to relate but right now your nerves are fraying at an alarming rate.

*If you try to jump-start the burial by kicking a few dirt clods into the hole and muttering "Good riddance," turn to page 70.*
*If you volunteer to rev up the Bobcat skid loader you noticed parked behind the caretaker's shed, turn to page 71.*
*If you shriek, "I admit the deed! Here, here! It is the beating of their hideous hearts!" fall to your knees and turn to page 72.*

Like a bored kid in a fabric store, your left leg twitches spastically and before you can stop its motion, you've kicked several dirt clods into the hole. They rattle and patter on the casket lid like fists pounding against it from inside. You scramble to the outer edge of the solemn gathering and mop nervous perspiration from your forehead. Your breathing comes in gasps. *Keep it together!* The preacher prays again and someone throws a bouquet into the hole.

Then everyone begins filing away. One or two of your cousins try to make eye contact as they pass and your mother gives you a strange look but you resolve to feign sorrow if confronted. No one speaks to you however and you soon find yourself alone with the man whose job it is to fill the hole.

You watch the other mourners drive away in their vehicles. When you scan the church parking lot, you see only your car now double parked next to nothing. Even the priest has departed. You become aware of your companion staring at you.

"I'm not supposed to do this with any of the family watching," he explains. "My wife said she'd have coffee and sandwiches on by two, so..."

"Yes, yes of course." You force a smile and totter past nearly two centuries of stone markers, pass through the cemetery gates and cross the empty road. The sound of the skid loader's engine roars to life just as you reach your car. You pause to steal a glance back.

What took hours to dig takes minutes to fill. The man waves amicably as he drives past in his rusty pickup when the job is done and you smile and return that wave. You feel as if a great burden has been lifted from you.

Relief gives way to elation as you realize that you've gotten away with murder (*probably second-degree, but still...*), apparent accidental infidelity AND the disposal of the body. Best of all, you got a measure of revenge on your creepy uncle and accomplished everything without arousing any suspicion.

You chuckle as you remember how your uncle looked with only one eyebrow. You wish you had had more time to finish that job, but overall you feel thrilled by today's events. You burst out laughing.

You're still chuckling as you slide into the driver's seat. You're snickering even as you repeatedly check your pockets for your car keys. You're still grinning at your reflection in the rear view mirror as you recall why you most recently held them.

But as you realize where you likely dropped the tiny utility knife and the ring of keys it was attached to...

That's when you stop smiling altogether.

# YOU DON'T KNOW JACK

## *Adrian Ludens*

The dead boy stood in the path twenty yards ahead. Jack pulled on the reins of his dun and the animal halted. The sun beat down mercilessly, and Jack paused to mop his brow with a threadbare red handkerchief. He rolled a quirley and surveyed his surroundings. To his left he saw only an endless expanse of rolling Dakota Territory prairie; to his right was more of the same. His direction took him toward the Black Hills, crouching on the distant horizon.

Jack squinted back at the ghost. Andy, eternally youthful, motioned with one transparent arm for the rider to leave the trail. Jack tugged on the reins and urged his horse in the direction his spectral companion pointed. The dun set off at a quick trot through the wild grass. Apparently satisfied, the spirit faded away. When Jack looked back at the spot where Andy had stood, he saw the reason for his brother's appearance. A prairie rattler, almost five feet long by Jack's estimation, moved along the trail in search of shade. Once they were far enough that Jack knew his horse wouldn't spook, he let the dun find its way back to the trail.

Three hours later, as the sun worked its way toward the horizon; Jack came upon the empty shell of an abandoned homestead. He appraised the structure. He felt played out and the way the dun's head hung, it needed rest also. But the winds from a storm had torn the roof off the dwelling long ago and it would afford him little shelter. Jack decided to continue on. Andy peered out from an empty window frame. He gazed at something in the scrub brush. Jack saw that it was a hoe, left behind by the homesteaders when they had moved on.

From the past, the sound of metal striking flesh echoed in Jack's ears. He grabbed the saddle's horn for balance and shook his head as if to keep the memory at bay. It was no use.

*"I'll race you, Jack!" Andy challenged and took off at a full sprint toward Rock Creek's main street. Jack let his younger brother get a good head start and then began to chase him. Twin plumes of dust marked the boys' progress, and then dissipated as they stood panting outside the post office. Their mother, referred to around town as "The Widow Woman," had sent the boys into Rock Creek from their farm to mail a letter. After their father's death, Mary had begun to correspond with kin back in Louisville. Unsure of how she would support herself and two boys here in the West, a move back to Kentucky seemed like the most practical option. It was Andy's job to mail the letter—a duty he attended to proudly. Jack was only along to supervise. He had no way of knowing he'd watch his little brother die that day.*

Jack looked toward the shell of the abandoned cabin, but Andy had faded away. Wearily, he picked up the reins. He was eager to leave the homestead—and the hoe—far behind. He wished he'd had to deal with the rattlesnake instead.

Three days passed as Jack slowly worked his way west.

The afternoon August sun found Jack approaching the foothills of the Black Hills. The imposing shape of Bear Butte loomed north of him; Fort Meade squatted to the south. Jack and the dun continued west and soon began to ascend the worn old mountains. The tall pines and spruce, spaced sporadically at first, began to thicken. Soon Jack was surrounded by trees. He felt peaceful, hidden. Only Andy interrupted Jack's solitude, occasionally appearing to point the way.

As they approached what the locals called Oyster Mountain, Andy appeared again, pointing at a small clear stream. The dun nickered happily at the prospect of water and rest and Jack contemplated making it their campsite for the night.

He removed the bridle from the dun and led it close to the stream. After he had tethered the horse securely in a location where the animal could drink and crop grass, he returned to the foot of the steep hill and squatted on his haunches. Jack gazed up at the rolling cloud banks and let his mind wander.

*After mailing the letter, Andy and Jack descended the post office stairs and paused in the street. This rare trip to town afforded them a measure of freedom and after a brief conference, they decided on a detour to the general store for some hard candy before starting on their way back. As they passed the Overland stagecoach station, the door flew open abruptly and a tall man dressed in buckskin stepped out, slamming the door behind him. Raucous laughter came from within. The young man scowled and hurried into the street, long hair bouncing on his shoulders with each stride. He moved toward them, clenching his fists in anger. Both boys recognized James, the new stagecoach stable hand, as he approached. It was Andy, in the innocence of youth, who greeted him.*

*"Mornin', Mr. Duck Bill," he greeted the approaching figure in the silly voice that never failed to give Jack the fits. Jack began to laugh but stopped when he saw James' eyes blaze and his face flush crimson. James uttered a strangled cry of rage and ran up a side street. He jumped a fence and landed in someone's meager garden. The boys gaped first at him, then at each other.*

*"You made him go plum crazy!" Jack chided his dumbstruck younger brother. "Why'd you go an' call him Duck Bill for?"*

*"That's what Mr. McCanles and the fellers at the stage coach station call him." Andy defended himself. "I was just bein' friendly."*

*"I don't think he likes that nickname," Jack said. "On account of his big nose."*

*Andy's eyes widened. "Jack, he's comin' back!"*

Something moved to Jack's left. Spooked, he made an awkward grab for his .45 caliber revolver. Andy's spectral form flickered before him. The spirit pointed toward the peak of the hill. Jack dutifully began to climb.

His boots slipped several times on the carpet of dry pine needles. The ascent was steeper than he had expected. The sun dipped below the horizon of the hills and as Jack climbed, the shadows lengthened and cool night air crept slyly across his face.

Near the top of Oyster Mountain, Jack approached an area where the pine needles and brush had been cleared away, exposing the dark earth. A sweat lodge constructed of thin tree branches and tanned buffalo hides sat in the center. The remains of a fire smoldered nearby and Jack saw one or two stones still heating amidst the embers. A lone Lakota stepped out of the sweat lodge and raised his hand in a somber greeting. "*How kola,*" he said as Jack approached. "Hello, friend."

"*How kola.* Call me Jack."

"*Micaje Nape Sica.*"

Jack shrugged and shook his head. The other man gave it to him in English. "My name is Bad Hand."

"Are you alone here, or are there others?"

"I am *esnella*—a loner. I come to *Paha Sapa* because my heart cries for a vision."

Jack grunted noncommittally.

"*Wachin ksapa yo,*" Bad Hand began. He paused and started again. "Listen to me." He gazed at the ground for a moment, carefully choosing his words. Then he resumed: "*Ki wanagi chikala,* the little spirit, came to me. My vision quest has already begun. He has asked me to share my *canupa,* my pipe, with you so that he may speak to you."

Bad Hand gestured for Jack to enter the sweat lodge. Jack wondered if it was Andy's ghost that had appeared before the Indian. Would he hear his brother's voice again after all these years?

"*Iyotaka,*" Bad Hand said when they were inside, motioning Jack to sit down. A shallow pit in the center of the enclosure was filled with hot stones from the fire outside. The heat was so fierce that Jack stripped off his shirt as he waited for his eyes to adjust to the dark interior. He sat as far from the heated stones as he could and Bad Hand positioned himself opposite him, pouring water onto the stones. Steam billowed and Jack fought the feeling of claustrophobia that welled within him. After several minutes, Bad Hand repeated the procedure with the water. He next removed a small clay pipe from a leather pouch and filled it with tobacco. Bad Hand chanted a prayer and smoked. Jack waited, sweating and thinking about Andy. Finally Bad Hand passed the pipe across the stones and sat back.

"You are on *ki wanagi tacaku*, the spirit path," Bad Hand announced.

Jack held the pipe and raised his eyebrows skeptically. "Already?"

"You follow *ki wanagi chikalathe*, the little spirit, do you not?"

"What little spirit?"

"The spirit of your brother. He wishes to speak to you. Smoke to cleanse your mind and then be still."

Jack raised the pipe to his lips with trembling hands. He had grown used to seeing Andy, but was this his chance to *hear* him again? Jack inhaled and immediately coughed the smoke back out. His lungs felt scorched. He inhaled again and his lungs cooled. He felt a sense of peace wash over him. Bad Hand closed his eyes and began a chant. He seemed to Jack to be very far away. Jack's ears hummed.

Jack sat still and tried to relax, but felt as if he were melting in the heat. Even in almost complete darkness, shadows seemed to flit around the sweat lodge. The humming sound increased until it became unbearable. Jack closed his eyes and covered his ears against the growing roar.

"...aaaaaaaaaaaaaaahhhhhAAACK!"

Then silence.

"Jack!" The speaker repeated urgently.

Jack opened his eyes and looked at his brother Andy. They were sitting together in a grassy field. The warm sun shone down, all benevolence.

"Hi, Jack."

Tears welled in Jack's eyes. "I miss you, Andy," he croaked.

"I'm tired. I wanna go home."

"Are you leaving me?"

"You have to let me go first. You being sad is what's keeping me here."

"But—"

"Let me rest."

"How am I s'posed to forget you?"

"You don't need to forget me." Andy rippled like a heat mirage. "But there's poison in your heart and you need to get rid of it."

"I don't understand."

"You'll know when the time is right to balance the scales." The ghost held up his small transparent pink hands in a weighing gesture. "I have learned a lot, stuck between two worlds. I will help you."

"Andy, wait. I'm sorry." Jack broke off, not knowing how to apologize. Wanting to say he wished it was him that had died instead. The specter faded away and Jack felt a wave of nausea wash over him like rancid pond scum. He closed his eyes.

When he opened them again, he found himself back in the sweat lodge. Bad Hand chanted across from him. As Jack looked, the other man's eyelids fluttered and opened.

Bad Hand crawled from the sweat lodge into the cool night air. Jack put on his shirt and followed. The temperature change was so drastic that Jack briefly wondered if he'd been entranced for months and had awoken in the dead of winter. He shivered uncontrollably for several minutes while his companion panted nearby.

"That's something I never want to do again," Jack said finally. "That was bad medicine."

Bad Hand jerked his head up, insulted.

"*Canl Waka,* coward!" he spat. "You must accept the visions the spirit brings you."

"Well, then I reckon I'm supposed to kill a man," Jack said dryly.

Bad Hand regarded him closely. "That is your *sintkala waksu*, your spirit path?"

"Yes. My brother Andy told me. He died when we were kids. Said I would know when the time was right for vengeance."

"My path rapidly approaches the clearing. Soon my spirit will go to *Mahpiya*, to Paradise. It will be a hot day. White men who are thirsty and tired of riding will run me down out of boredom and anger."

Jack didn't know the right words to say, so he kept silent.

"I have done no wrong," Bad Hand said. "My heart is good. Let *Wakan Tanka* come for me."

"I didn't have much schooling," Jack began, "but I know a raw deal when I see one. If what you say about bein' killed is true, then I'm sorry. I don't know why you were named Bad Hand, but pardner, it sounds like you been dealt one."

Jack fell asleep beneath the stars and woke beneath the sun. He sat up and rubbed his eyes. His muscles shrieked in protest and his joints felt stiff from spending the night sprawled on the earth. Bad Hand and the sweat lodge were gone. Jack wondered briefly if the other man had really been there at all.

He descended and drank deeply from the stream. Then he saddled up and rode deeper into the Black Hills. Jack urged his mount to the southwest, through Boulder Canyon. Andy appeared only when Jack began to wander off course. To the south, Granite Peak rose and sank behind them as they progressed. Jack rode to the top of a hill and was surprised by an expanse of meadow. The view, with Whitewood Peak to the north and Pillar Peak to the south, took his breath away. They rested briefly, Jack gnawing on jerked venison from his pack while the dun contentedly cropped the tall grass. He pondered his brother's words and slipped back again. Back to Kansas, and to Andy sprinting away in fear.

*James thundered toward them, bright blue eyes blazing. The fringe of his buckskin bounced in time with his shoulder length hair. He was brandishing a garden hoe, stolen from a nearby garden. Its iron head gleamed in the sun. Andy turned and fled, but in his terror, he chose the path that eventually led home, rather than toward the potential protection of other townsfolk. Jack felt as if he were rooted to the earth. Where was everyone? Didn't anyone hear what was happening? It was only after James had bounded past him that fear for his brother outstripped his fear for himself. Jack spun and trailed after them.*

*In any race between a man in his early twenties and a nine-year-old boy, the boy always wins. This is because the older man allows the boy to win. This day, however, the man doing the running didn't care to observe that unspoken rule.*

*As Jack watched, helpless to intercede, James swung the hoe in a long arc. It connected with Andy's head and Jack heard the sound that he could never forget. Andy's small body sprawled to the ground in a cloud of dust.*

It was afternoon again by the time Jack and his horse forded the stream in Spruce Gulch and began the slow ascent of another wooded hill. The wind and trees had conspired to play a trick on Jack and when he crested the next hill, he was met with a startling cacophony of sounds. The dun tossed its head with disapproval as Jack gaped at the settlement below. The bustling cavalcade of activity at the bottom of the hill nearly overwhelmed the senses.

Men shouted, laughed and called to one another. Grubby miners, cursing and spitting, led pack mules through the muddy, rutted streets. Dusty cowhands tilted their heads to look up at the kept women who flirted from the windows of their rooms. Some of the men turned away while others shuffled toward the brothel doors, looking both excited and foolish. A small group of men and women clotted one street corner as a tall man in black robes stood on a barrel and preached to his flock. Chinese men smiled obsequiously and pulled their carts, disappearing like ants into dark passageways. The tinkle of a piano came from one saloon. The bat-wing doors of another suddenly burst open and a barkeep and a sunburned cowboy tossed a dapper looking gambler into the dust. One or two respectable women of society ventured along the streets, while legitimate businessmen and con artists smoked cigars and eyed each other shrewdly. A group of Lakota Indians, in town for the day to trade, made an eye-catching spectacle of buckskin and feathers. Standing there in the midst of it all, looking up at Jack with supernatural clarity, stood Andy.

Jack sighed and started down the hill, following his spirit path straight into the heart of the mountain mining town.

After securing a stall for his horse in one of the outlying stables, Jack spent most of the hot July afternoon exploring the boom town. Andy had disappeared again as Jack was descending the hill so Jack wandered, doing his best not to idle anywhere too long. He didn't need anyone pegging him for a deadbeat. He browsed the mercantile, stopped for a questionable-tasting whiskey at one of the many saloons, and waved a good-natured dismissal toward a busty, toothless matron who was attempting to solicit clients from her windowsill.

Jack got a closer look at the tall bearded preacher as he exhorted his makeshift congregation. The preacher caught Jack's eyes and addressed him directly. "What brings you here, my son?"

"I want to help my brother find peace," Jack explained.

The preacher stretched out his arms and took in the crowd with a beatific gaze. "This man is here to help his brother," he cried. "That is what our Savior asks of all of us: to help one another!" Applause and scattered murmurs of approval came from the small crowd, and Jack took advantage of the moment to slip away down the street. Behind him Jack heard the preacher continue his sermon. "In Ecclesiastes, chapter four, Solomon writes..."

Jack kept wandering through the crowds searching for Andy, or for some sign of the man he needed to kill. He found neither. It was early in the evening now, with menacing dark thunderclouds rapidly rolling in from the north. A chilly gust of wind spat dust in his eyes. They watered as he hurried up the street. A rumble of thunder goaded several pedestrians into picking up their respective paces.

The sky overhead soon darkened and the first drops of rain splattered in the dust. The bare ground would soon become a quagmire and wagons jostled hurriedly up and down the streets. The horses pranced and reared nervously as the thunder increased in frequency and ferocity. People hurried indoors. The saloons and stores were suddenly filled to capacity. Miners scurried to their tent camps. The wind whipped at Jack as he sought shelter and he grabbed the front brim of his cowboy hat to stop it from blowing away.

Jack had a vague idea of heading for the nearest hotel when Andy appeared in the dimness of an adjacent alley. He stood with his hands behind his back and he seemed to gaze expectantly at his still-living brother. Jack turned and sprinted in Andy's direction.

Just ahead Jack saw wooden steps descending alongside the building. Looking down, he saw the ghostly white face of his brother floating in the darkness below. The sky opened and rain began to drench the earth. Jack hurried down the stairs into the darkness below.

Andy was not waiting at the bottom of the steps, so Jack pushed open a red-painted wooden door. He stepped into a dark stone passageway, lit by lanterns hung on nails from the walls every twenty yards or so. Jack moved cautiously along the chilly passage. A rumbling sound came from somewhere in the darkness ahead. Suddenly the silhouette of a man emerged. As the figure approached, Jack was able to make him out more clearly. A small Chinese man pulled a wooden cart filled with carefully folded garments. The Chinese man showed no indication of slowing down as he approached and Jack was about to turn around and hurry back to the door when the little man executed a sharp turn and disappeared down a corridor Jack hadn't noticed. The rumble of the cart's wheels faded away and Jack heard only the gentle hiss of the oil lamps and the distant rumble of thunder.

Why had Andy guided him here? Just to get him out of the rain? Jack knew there had to be more to it than that. As quietly as he could, he stepped toward the tunnel the Chinese launderer had taken. Unconsciously holding his breath, he peered cautiously around the corner.

"Why you make so much noise?" a sharp voice complained from behind him and Jack jolted in surprise. He spun around and saw a wizened old Chinese man standing in the opposite passageway. The elderly man wore a shimmery black jacket embroidered with white thread. His dark eyes seemed to flicker in the gas light and a long white mustache hung like cobwebs from both sides of his thin mouth.

"I am Shen Liu. You are late," he continued curtly, like a schoolmarm admonishing a tardy student. "Come."

The Chinese man turned and moved down a passage so small that Jack had to stoop in order to enter. Jack followed the old man down the pitch-black tunnel. His guide told him when to turn left or right or when there was a step up or down. After a period of prolonged silence, Jack began to feel claustrophobic.

"Where are you taking me?" Jack muttered. "I'm a cowpuncher, not a miner searching for the mother lode."

Suddenly a hand grabbed the back of Jack's collar and hauled him backwards into a dimly lit den. Jack spun around and reached for his revolver but was shocked to find his holster empty. On the verge of panic, Jack realized it was Shen Liu standing in front of him.

"You very slow," the Chinese man said. He handed back the gun. Jack took it, stupefied. The old man gestured toward a luxuriant rug. "Sit."

Jack eased himself to the floor and sat cross-legged before a wooden tray. The tray itself was elaborately decorated with ivory inlays and pearlescent seashells. Atop the wooden tray were a variety of items including two smaller metal trays; a tiny oil lamp; a pipe with a bamboo stem; and a blue and white porcelain bowl. The old man sat down across from Jack.

"Your brother came to me yesterday as I smoked," Shen Liu said as he trimmed the wick on the little oil lamp. "His round white face and black eyes nearly scared the life from me."

"At least there's still some life left in you to scare," Jack remarked.

The old man filled a pipe using something that looked to Jack like a skeleton key with a tiny spoon at one end.

"An-dee is his name?"

Jack nodded.

"He speak of the sorrow you and him share." Shen Liu held the pipe over the flame burning in the lamp. "He ask me to help you."

The old man raised his pipe to his lips and inhaled deeply. He closed his eyes and his shoulders sank as he relaxed.

"We build tunnels for laundry, but have many secret places as well." The old man arched an eyebrow slyly. Jack glanced around the dimly lit alcove.

"Bill, ready to pay," Shen Liu continued. Jack concentrated, trying to follow the old man's words. *What had he said? A bill needed to be paid?*

Shen Liu held the pipe out to Jack. He took it and tentatively inhaled. Rather than making him cough, the smoke was thick and sweet. It felt like molasses coating his lungs. Jack felt the tension flow from his body.

Shen Liu held the pipe over the flame. Then he returned it to Jack who put the small pipe to his lips and inhaled again. The room tilted sharply and Jack toppled onto the rug, his limbs felt simultaneously weightless and unbearably heavy. He thought he heard Andy singing a song they had learned as children. Jack was dimly aware of the old Chinese man retiring to a corner of the room. The opium was a shock to Jack's system. He thought he saw someone else in the room but the presence always flitted just out of his field of vision.

"Aces and eights are the most important cards in a deck." Andy's voice seemed to come from nowhere and everywhere. "I also like the number ten."

Jack scarcely dared to breathe as he concentrated on his dead brother's child-like ramblings.

"One shot."

The sound of flies buzzing around his ears woke him and Jack sat up, groggily rubbing his eyes. The bedsprings creaked in protest as he rolled over and swung his legs onto the floor. Jack noticed a water pitcher and a glass on a battered dresser. He walked over, ignored the glass and gratefully gulped the liquid straight from the pitcher. Jack shook his head, trying to clear it. Scattered images of the previous night paraded through his memory: the Chinese laundry tunnels, Shen Liu, the opium pipe and Andy's cryptic words.

*Jack screamed his brother's name as he ran to where Andy lay. He slid to the ground and gathered his brother in his arms. James dropped the hoe absently, his bright blue eyes showing a mixture of fear and gratification. Jack rocked Andy in his arms. He palmed a trickle of blood from his brother's cheek and began to sob. He knew he was too old to cry, but this was different. He cried for his brother, lying so still. He cried when he thought about breaking the news to their mother. And he cried because he had no father to break the news to.*

Jack gulped the rest of the water. His hand trembled so violently that he dribbled most of what was left down the front of his shirt. Then Jack grabbed his boots from their place beside the bed and pulled them on. He buckled on his holster, grabbed his hat and descended the stairs. Jack stopped at the desk to inquire about payment. The desk clerk, a tall man with spectacles and carefully oiled and combed hair, informed Jack that "an old Chinaman" had brought him in and paid for the room the night before. The clerk volunteered to hold the room if Jack intended to return.

"Much obliged," Jack told the clerk. He left the lobby and stepped into the bright noonday sun. Jack rambled up and down the streets of the bustling town, casually taking in the sights, but always on the lookout for Andy or the man he needed to find. About mid-afternoon, Jack stepped into a restaurant for a bite to eat. He ordered liver and onions and Arbuckle's coffee. As Jack paid he realized he was dangerously low on funds. He'd have to find work, and soon. Maybe tonight he could win a few hands of poker to get him by for a few more days.

On his way out, Jack asked the man running the place where the best spots for poker were. "Every saloon in town has games running every night," the ruddy-faced man said, scratching at his scalp. "Seems like a lot of the high rollers make an appearance over at the No. 10."

Jack raised his eyebrows. "Number ten?"

"Sure. Nuttal and Mann's Saloon No. 10."

Jack headed outside thinking that he might try his hand against a few of these so-called "high rollers." He stepped into the street and stopped short.

Andy had said something about the number ten. Jack's eyes narrowed and he turned and marched purposefully down Main Street.

Jack almost missed his intended destination. The sign hanging from the saloon was small and unassuming. As Jack approached, a grubby miner burst through a set of bat-wing doors and stuck a filthy finger in Jack's face. He seemed about to speak, but before he could, a brawny barkeep grabbed the miner by the collar and tossed him into the dirt.

"Don't mind him; he's full as a tick," the barkeep said to Jack.

"I see that."

"Name's Harry Young," the barkeep said as he opened one of the doors to go back inside. "I run a tight ship here at the No. 10."

His stomach tightening in a way he did not quite understand, Jack followed the man inside.

A few hours later Jack found himself gazing at his brother's killer.

The man had arrived at the No. 10 amidst the admiring looks of nearly everyone in and around the bar. James was a hard man to miss, standing several inches above most others. His long wavy hair spilled onto a buckskin fringed coat and a scraggly handlebar mustache diminished the appearance of his protruding nose and petulant lips.

Someone bought James a drink. He downed it in a gulp and stationed himself near one of the tables. Sensing that the tall man wanted in, one of the players threw in his hand and vacated his chair. Jack was surprised when Andy appeared in the empty seat. Yet no one else noticed. Andy stared directly at Jack, his eyes dull and hollow. Then the big gambler dropped into the chair and obliterated the apparition.

The symbolism was not lost on Jack, who seethed as the cards flew.

Andy's killer had achieved a great deal of notoriety in recent years. Everyone referred to the tall man not as James, but a different name. Jack didn't know if it was a nickname or an alias. He wondered if James had changed his name after fleeing Rock Creek. Jack's blood ran cold as he watched the tall man handle his cards.

Jack hovered, tossing back occasional whiskey shots and steeling his nerve. When another of the players dropped out, Jack stepped forward and took his place.

"Reckon I know you," Jack addressed Andy's killer as the cards were dealt.

"Reckon everybody does," the tall man shot back and the room erupted in laughter. Both men eyed their cards. Jack kept a pair of tens and discarded his three undesirables. His new cards amounted to nothing and he folded. The man to Jack's left discarded a pair of cards and the dealer, sitting to Jack's right, tossed him two more.

"Mebbe you remember me from Rock Creek, Kansas," Jack pressed.

James looked up.

Jack expected to see the shock of recognition in the other man's eyes. Successful gambler that he was, however, James' facial features and body language betrayed no reaction.

"Never been there," he said.

Without breaking eye contact, James tossed one card and received another. He tossed a coin into the pot. The dealer stayed and tossed in his coin. The player to Jack's left folded.

James raised. The dealer called.

"Straight," James said, fanning his cards.

"Beats my two pair," the dealer admitted, and James swept up the pot.

So went the evening and much of the night. The tall man continued playing to the gallery, cracking jokes and accepting free drinks. Jack won a few small pots but kept playing and soon found he was dead broke. He pushed back his chair and stood, fuming. Feeling desperate, but not knowing what to do, he headed for the bat-wing doors. He had to get outside, gather his wits...

*Andy lay in Jack's arms, lifeless as a log.*

*Jack shot beseeching looks in every direction. The only living person he saw was James shuffling back towards town. Seized by a sudden fury, Jack screamed.*

*"I'll kill you when I grow up! If I ever see you again I will KILL YOU!"*

*James did not turn around. Instead, he returned to town, mounted the first horse he found and immediately fled Kansas.*

"Hey, puncher!"

Jack stopped short. The voice belonged to James.

"I feel awful about fleecing you," the gambler said, amid snickers from several onlookers. "Let me pay for dinner tonight and breakfast tomorrow." James tossed a couple coins in Jack's direction.

Reflexively, Jack caught the arcing coins.

"I'll be right here tomorrow night," James said, still looking at Jack. Now his eyes seemed to burn with secret meaning. "If you decide to settle accounts."

Jeering laughter chased Jack out into the darkness. His blood pounded in his temples as he staggered through the humid night air. He hurried across the still-muddy street and ducked into the shadows between two buildings.

Jack suddenly realized that James, unlike the others, hadn't been laughing. He stood pondering this. Perhaps Jack wasn't the only tortured soul haunted by the past. He tried to imagine James tossing and turning through sleepless nights. He wondered if the other man ever saw Andy's face in nightmares or during waking hours.

Jack found his way back to the same hotel and gave the desk clerk the coins.

He clutched at the banister as he ascended the stairs, his brain swimming with unanswered questions. Inside the room, Jack kicked off his boots, took off his gun belt and collapsed onto the mattress.

It seemed as if the gambler's voice echoed in Jack's ears all night long. *"I'll be right here tomorrow night if you decide to settle accounts."*

Jack's mouth was dry as he slipped into the Saloon No. 10 the next night. He moved down the bar, stopping a few steps away from a table of poker players. He stood directly behind the man who had killed his brother. Several others were gathered around the table, taking a look at the hands that were dealt.

James raised his cards and Jack saw that the top one was a jack. Jack realized the face on the card bore an eerie resemblance to his own image. Then he noticed that the other cards in James' hand were all aces and eights. Andy's words came back to Jack with chilling clarity.

James sat very still, doing nothing with his cards, and Jack realized the big man was waiting for him. *Waiting for me to settle accounts. Balance the scales.* Andy flickered in and out of view beside the table. His eyes gazed longingly upward at something that Jack could not see.

Knowing the time was right Jack raised his Colt .45 and aimed the barrel directly at James Butler Hickok's back. Before anyone could react, Jack McCall pulled the trigger and finally set his brother's spirit free.

# MIM'S ROOM

## *C. W. LaSart*

"Mim?" I asked one day, many years ago. "Do you ever wish you were normal?"

"What's normal?" she said. "I think the word you are looking for is 'average', and in all my years, I have never once known a person who strove to be average."

I get what she was saying, but I can't help but think she may have answered differently if she'd known how things were going to end up.

I wasn't allowed in Mim's room on the night that the rich woman came to her for help, but she told me what happened a few days later. After we heard that the woman was dead. I remember feeling stunned as I listened, as much by the look on Mim's face as by the tale she told. I had never known Mim to have anything less than a smile on her face, a joyful countenance that subtracted decades from her true age. But that night, there was no smile. The worry and guilt etched lines in her face that I had never seen. The weight of guilt over the woman's death rested so heavily upon her shoulders as to be almost visible.

Mim felt responsible for that woman's death, and I guess in a way, she was. But it wound up even, since the woman was also the reason that Mim died, though if anyone should shoulder the actual responsibility, I guess it would be me.

We came to live with Mim shortly after my father's death. He was killed in an accident, somewhere across the North Dakota border. He was a truck driver and the roads were icy that night. My mother doesn't talk about it much and the casket was closed, so I guess it must've been pretty bad. I remember his truck, though. It was purple and I loved it. I loved him too. It was my tenth birthday.

Mim lived all the way across the state, but there was little choice as to whether we would move or not. There wasn't enough money to support Mom and me, and Mim was doing okay financially. She was an artist, living comfortably off her paintings, though her art never saw a frame, was never hung in a gallery. She never even sold the paintings, which I thought was strange, but I would learn soon enough how Mim made her living. About the magic in the family bloodline that kept food on the table.

My memories of Mim had always been positive, though I had only visited her a few times as a child. I remember Mom and Dad would fight quite a bit before we'd go see her and I couldn't understand why Dad didn't like Mim. She was so nice and accommodating on our rare visits. I asked Mom about it once and she told me he didn't approve of Mim. I could tell by her tone that she really didn't either. That was another thing I would figure out later. It wasn't disapproval that made the relationship between mother and daughter so strained. It was fear. My mother was afraid of my grandmother, and my father was as well. Almost everyone was afraid of Mim, but it seemed so silly to me as a little girl. It still does.

I was an artist too and Mim was very supportive of my talent in a way that my mother was not. I remember Mom telling someone that toddlers weren't supposed to be capable of drawing a complete circle until three years of age, but I was drawing smiley faces, complete with hair and ears by eighteen months. Her tone had been more wary than proud, as if she was suspicious of my talent. By ten I was sketching portraits with a talent that few adults possessed. I remember how Mim would fawn over my drawings, taking the time to coach me in areas I was lacking. Overjoyed with my abilities, she did what she could to foster them, which seemed to make my mother withdraw further from us both. I didn't mind all that much. Mom had always been a bit cold, less affectionate than other mothers. But Mim was great, hugging me regularly and paying attention to me. I loved being around her. She became a bright light in my dreadful existence after the death of my father.

Mim lived in a modest house on the edge of town, surrounded by dark forest and crowned with a beautiful flower garden. She lived just far enough out that it felt like the country, but close enough to be only be a few minutes' drive to the store and for the city plows to clear the road in the winter. We moved there in June and the garden was the most glorious thing I'd ever seen. So many colors and scents. It became like my own fairyland.

We each had our own room and the run of the house except the back bedroom. That was Mim's room, where she did her work and met her clients. I wasn't allowed in there initially, but it didn't really bother me. I had my own room which was easily twice the size of my room before, and I had the garden. I didn't need anything else.

It was shortly before school started that I discovered what made Mim and me so different from others. I was sitting in the garden sketching, as was my habit, and Mom and Mim sat close by on the porch swing, enjoying the mild weather. Almost finished with my sketch, I sat back to enjoy it. In the picture, a little girl (who was actually me) sat in a similar position with a pad of paper. Thousands of butterflies swirled around her, many lighting upon her upturned face and outstretched hands.

I'd selected a patch of yard close to the rose bushes and as I sat there a butterfly flitted upon a nearby rose. Reaching out to scoop it up in my hand, I was instead rewarded with the prick of a thorn, a bead of blood welling upon my finger. Frustrated, I grabbed my pad of paper and made to get up, intending to find a bandage in the medicine chest in the bathroom, but I stopped short as my blood smeared the picture I had spent most of the morning sketching. Tears filled my eyes and I tried to wipe the red smudge away, but it was no good and I only managed to spread it further.

"Look, Mim. I've ruined it." I held the picture out to my Mom and Mim in disgust, puzzled as my Mom paled and Mim sat forward with earnest attention.

The sky grew momentarily darker as if a cloud had passed before the sun and as I turned my head to look, I realized it was no ordinary cloud. Butterflies, thousands of them, came fluttering into the yard, so many that it was hard to see across the street. They swirled around me, many landing upon my hands as I reached out in amazement. I remember giggling as their tiny feet tickled my skin, but my joy was short-lived. Just then Mom stood up with a curse and turned her back on me, but not before I saw the tears in her eyes. She walked into the house without another word and Mim hugged me tight, her face beaming with pride.

After that I was allowed in Mim's room.

"The magic's in the blood," Mim said to me as I sat upon her massive bed later that night, my vision awash with the grandeur of her room. There was a sitting table against one wall with two ornate chairs, and an easel in the corner, situated on a drop cloth that had seen so many paint splatters that the original color was indeterminable. Tubes of paint in various states of use lay scattered upon a small tray near the easel. But mostly there were paintings. Too many paintings to count. They lay piled upon almost every flat surface and still others leaned in piles up against the walls and the furniture. Every shape and size was present. Every imaginable scenario was displayed upon those canvases. I saw paintings of men in business suits sitting at desks, paintings of small children holding hands with angels. Even a painting of a dog lying on a vet's exam table, its body twisted but the owner smiling beside it. Each with a rusty smudge of dried blood in the corner.

I didn't understand all those paintings and I told Mim so.

"All in good time, my child," she said, patting my hand. "You have a gift, but it will take time to understand it. It's a gift that has been passed down for generations in the women of our family. It's different for all of us. I paint, you draw. My mother was an amazing sculptor. I'm not really sure why it skipped your mother; she could never draw more than a stick figure in her life. But you have it, baby. And I think it's strong in you. I will help you learn how to use it."

Mim said that it was a gift from God, so we had to try to never use it for evil. I asked if she ever had used it for bad purposes and she said no, but a look in her eyes told me she might be lying. I let it drop. It didn't matter. I asked if it was wrong for her to accept money for her gift, but she said everyone used what God gave them to get by, and she didn't see why we had to be any different. People paid her a lot of money to help them get what they wanted and it seemed like a fine living to me.

We were up all night and I went to bed when the birds were singing, my head full of stories and forbidden knowledge. I felt special for the first time in my life and I had a bond with Mim that I had lacked with my own Mom. I was a bit afraid, overwhelmed by what I'd learned, but I was truly happy as well, for the first time that I could remember.

It didn't take a genius to realize that the people in town were afraid of Mim. Even the ones who were nice to her seemed grateful when she finally walked away, sometimes breathing an audible sigh of relief. That fear soon extended to me, leaving me an outcast at school. They didn't bully me, or pick on me, but I was a creature to be avoided, whispered about behind my back. I didn't care much. I had Mim. I didn't need other friends.

Mim and I had a special connection, though she said we weren't truly psychic.

"I'm a natural broadcaster," she explained one afternoon. "And you're a natural receiver. My thoughts are strong and you're sensitive to them, which is why we can sometimes talk without moving our mouths. Real psychics, they can hear most everyone. We aren't like that, you and I, but we have a special bond."

From almost day one I could hear Mim in my head. She was a source of comfort when I felt troubled, advice when I felt conflicted. I think she could hear some of my thoughts as well, or she was just sensitive to my emotions, because she was always there in my head when I needed her. Hearing Mim in my head is probably what I miss the most now that she is gone. It's so lonely in there. Just me. I wish I could hear her. Maybe soon I will hear her again.

Whether Mim let me watch her work or not depended on the job.. If it was something like a man wanting a loan from the bank, I sat quietly on her bed while she talked to the person and collected her fee. When they were gone she would pull up a chair next to her easel and let me watch her paint. Her hands moved so fast, the scene forming at a startling rate. Sometimes when the mood really struck her, she would drop her paintbrush and dig in with her fingers, the swirls and dots left behind forming beautiful art that no one else would ever see.

Some people sent thank you letters when their desires came true, some sent scolding messages if it didn't turn out the way they had imagined, still others never contacted her again. Mim always made a point to tell people that the magic might not work the way they thought it should, or sometimes not work at all. She warned them that she couldn't control it, merely gave it a place to start. No one ever seemed too concerned that it might go wrong. They all paid the fee happily, certain they would soon get what they wanted. People are greedy. Most of them wanted money, or fame, but a few came with selfless reasons. There were always the ones who were praying for their child to live, or their spouse, or parent.

My favorite painting in Mim's room was one clearly done by finger. It showed a little boy lying asleep in a hospital bed, a luminous angel at his side, her hand resting upon his brow. I asked Mim if the boy had been cured, and she smiled sadly, telling me that he had. I asked why she looked like that and she told me he was killed in a car accident a year later. She said that sometimes death can't be fooled. It could be put off for a while, but sometimes it came back for what was rightfully its own. She told me something that day that I will never forget. Even then, at the tender age of twelve or thirteen, I knew it was important.

"Baby," she said, cupping my chin in her soft hand. "Sometimes bad things happen to good people. And sometimes, no matter how good your intentions are, the deeds of well-meaning people are to blame. We need to do our best not to cause harm to others, but when it happens, whether we meant it or not, we must accept responsibility for our part of their pain."

Over the years I have learned a lot from Mim. She always encouraged me to practice my drawing, sometimes letting me try to make small things happen, but never letting me do any actual jobs for her. She said I was too young. I wasn't ready. Mim knew so much more than me. I always trusted her advice. I tried to be obedient, to never stretch my wings beyond where she allowed, but sometimes I just wanted something so badly, I would break the rules. Mim's silent disapproval always hurt much worse than my mom's yelling.

One thing I've noticed in all this time is that Mim never used the power for herself. Not once did she paint her desires, her needs. No matter how things were going,

I never saw a painting that directly benefited her other than the payment she received for her work.

I wonder if I've made a mistake. I guess it's too late now.

The real trouble started with a visit from a woman named Monica St. George. I was used to strangers coming and going at all hours, usually paid little attention to the visitors to Mim's room, but Monica was different. She was by far the richest person I had ever seen, her clothes and jewelry finer than anything in my experience. Her hair looked like it was professionally done, her make-up (something I had only recently become interested in) exquisite. There was something in her bearing as well; the way she walked seemed almost *regal*. She was definitely someone who was used to getting everything she wanted. I knew who she was only because *everyone* in town did. She was as close to a celebrity as our town could come, being the much younger wife of the richest man in the area. It was a fact that Nathaniel St. George owned half the businesses around, but it was also whispered that he had connections to the mob and was hiding in the Midwest to avoid the Feds.

I wanted to go in with her, to see what it was that this woman could possibly want from Mim, since I knew it couldn't be money, but Mim had told me to stay in the living room and locked the bedroom door. I tried to eavesdrop for a while, but the wood was too thick, their tones too hushed. Forty-five minutes later, the door opened and Monica St. George left without so much as a sideways glance at me. I could tell she'd been crying, but her jaw was stiff, her expensive makeup still in place, only the redness of her eyes and nose gave her away.

A few days later, Mim called me into her room. I wasn't sure what she wanted, but I knew it must be serious, she looked very grave. I worried that she'd discovered my drawings of Stephen, a boy in school that I desperately wanted to go on a date with, but it was nothing so simple. She shut the door so my mother wouldn't hear, and sat upon the bed next to me, taking my hand in hers.

"Baby, I did something wrong. I didn't mean to, but something terrible has happened and it's my fault," she said, her blue eyes welling with tears.

"What is it, Mim? I'm sure it was an accident."

"Monica St. George died." The tears spilled over; trailing down her cheeks in muddy tracks (Mim's makeup wasn't nearly the quality of Ms. St. George's).

"How did she die?" My mind was spinning, trying to find a connection between my loving grandmother and this rich woman's death. No matter how hard I tried, I couldn't conceive of an instance that would result in Mim being responsible for her demise.

Mim said nothing, standing and retrieving a painting from her closet. She set it on the easel in front of me and let me stare at it for a long time before speaking. I wasn't completely sure what I was seeing, but the painting was awful. It depicted Monica St. George in a bed, her face twisted in pain. A large pool of blood was very bright against the sheets between her legs; her spread thighs smeared with gore.

"A miscarriage." Mim put the painting back in the closet and returned to my side; the lines her face making her look older, tired. It was the first time that I'd ever really given any thought to hold old Mim was and it terrified me.

"Why?"

"She was pregnant. She feared that the baby belonged to another man, not her husband. She was worried the child would be born black, and her husband would know she'd been unfaithful with one of their servants. An abortion was out of the question; Nathaniel would've found out. So she came to me to lose the baby before she was far enough along that he could know. I guess she died from complications."

I was stunned. Mim had always told me that I must never use my gift for evil intent, must never do anything that meant taking the life of another, or getting what someone else deserved. I felt betrayed. Mim looked away from my face, her shame apparent in her posture. She looked defeated, beaten. I knew in that moment that Mim wasn't exactly the person I thought I knew, not the person who I had spent the last many years idolizing. I know now that this is something we all deal with while growing up; realizing the adults in our lives aren't perfect, but in that moment I was angry at her. I wasn't mad for what she'd done, I was furious that she wasn't who I thought she was, who I'd built her up to be.

The cool period between Mim and myself felt like it lasted a lifetime, but in truth it was only a few days. I got a call that weekend from Stephen. It seemed the drawings had worked. The next night I had my first date and I couldn't have been happier. I quickly forgot my anger at Mim.

There's something outside. I can hear a dog howling in the night and the sounds of branches breaking in the yard. The house is so quiet. I'm afraid, but excited. Did it work?

My mother had been working the night shift at a die casting factory for about a year, and she was working the night that Mim died. Stephen and I had just gone out for a movie (our third date, though for the life of me I can't remember what we saw) and I returned home in a haze of happiness. Stephen asked me to prom. I couldn't believe it. After years of being a loner, being the last one picked in gym class, utterly ignored in the halls of the school, I officially had a boyfriend and he was taking me to prom. I couldn't have been giddier as I rushed through the garden, eager to tell Mim my news. My excitement faded as I neared the house, noticing the front door was open to the night.

"Mim?" I called, stepping into the foyer and around a toppled table. The place was a mess, papers scattered everywhere, broken glass twinkling on the floor in the lamplight. Mim said nothing. I thought about running back down the driveway, chasing Stephen's car in hopes he would see me and stop, but I couldn't leave without knowing where Mim was. Knowing that she was okay.

I tried to be quiet, certain that whoever had done this awful thing to our house was still there, hiding in a dark corner, waiting for me with bated breath. But all thoughts of silence left my mind when I found her.

Mim was in the kitchen. She lay among the shattered dishes, crumpled, beaten. There was more blood than I had ever seen in my life. I knelt beside her, careful not to cut myself on the glass, and felt for a pulse, though now that I look back on it; it was a foolish thing to do. She was obviously dead. She'd been beaten so badly that I almost didn't recognize her face, her skull misshapen by the blows, one cloudy eye forced from the socket until it lay upon her purple cheek. Her neck was bent at an odd angle, the empty eye socket glared up at me with reproach. *I hadn't been there for her.* If I had been there, maybe I could've stopped it. Maybe she even knew it was my fault.

I don't remember what happened after that. I think I called someone. It could've been my mother, or maybe it was the police. There was a lot of commotion; I have vague recollections of about a million people rushing in, people in uniforms, the dark shirts of the police officers, the white gloves of the paramedics. I can still hear a gentle voice in my head, telling me it was time to *"let her go"*, though I don't know how long I'd been holding her hand. Her skin felt cold. I remember that. They'd covered her with a sheet too, but blooms of blood had soaked through, like the red poppies that she grew in the garden.

We stayed at a hotel until the investigation was over. I awoke every night screaming, my Mom soothing me, begging me to be quiet before they kicked us out. When we returned to the house, it had been cleaned by professionals, all traces of blood gone from the floor and walls, though they missed a splatter on the ceiling. Mom had to get the ladder out of the shed to clean it. In the end, I think she may have just painted over it.

My life became little more than dark snatches of reality, I retained nothing but the nightmare of what it was, though when I closed my eyes, I still saw her there, that dangling blue eye growing dry against her cool cheek.

Stephen called the following week and told me he was going to prom with someone else. I don't think I even responded, just hung the phone up while he tried to explain. It didn't matter. I didn't deserve to be happy. I didn't deserve anything. Not while Mim was lowered into her grave and a handful of townspeople watched. Not while my head was silent, Mim's warm thoughts no longer mingling with my own. I wished it had been me. I still do.

When I was younger, Mim and I used to spend most evenings in her room, me drawing while she painted. I remember the laughter we would share and how excited she would act over each picture I did. But that's gone now. Mother has forbidden me from entering the room, would be outraged if she knew I still spent my evenings there while she worked. She also forbade me from drawing anything that wasn't school-related, but that has been an easy rule to uphold. I haven't felt like drawing anything until tonight.

It's been almost two months since Mim was killed. The police say they have no leads, are calling it a botched burglary, but Mom and I know better. It was Nathaniel St. George, or whatever men he hires to do such deeds. It was payback for his young wife. Restitution for her death. Mom doesn't know how he found out, but I do.

I don't know why I told Stephen about it. I'm not sure if I wanted to be more interesting or if I just needed to share it with someone outside the family, but I did and I can't take it back now. Who knows, maybe that's the only reason he even asked me out, to know what sort of things we witches were up to on the edge of town. I'm certain he told others and it got back to St. George. Now Mim is dead and it's all my fault.

My grandfather died long before I was born, the victim of an accident much like my own dad. Mim never remarried, though she was an attractive woman, choosing to live out the rest of her life single, raising my mother alone in her house on the edge of town. I found an old wedding photo of her and Granddad, though. It's amazing how beautiful she was. That's how I chose to draw her, beautiful and young, no trace of the injuries that took her life. She's smiling in the picture I sketched, her arms held out to me for an embrace. I think it may be the finest thing I've ever drawn, except for the smudge of rusty blood in the corner.

I can hear her again; she's back in my head, though her presence feels different now. It's not warm and welcome like it used to be. At first I wasn't sure it was her at all, the voice is different, cold and gravelly, but I know now that it's her and that the drawing worked. I'm afraid of the things she's saying; they're dark and scary words, things that Mim never would have thought before, but I guess she has a right to be angry with me.

I'm scared. I can hear something moving about the house, the slow shuffle of feet, the scrape of furniture being bumped. Part of me wishes I hadn't done it. Wishes I had left well enough alone, but I owe Mim an apology. I need to tell her I didn't mean any of this to happen. She owes me an explanation as well. For the painting I found buried in her closet. The painting of a purple truck, just like my Dad's, crumpled in a heap at the bottom of a

ravine. The driver was not much more than a hunk of meat visible through the shattered windshield. Maybe she can forgive me if I forgive her?

I can hear the sounds in the hall now. Shuffling, squelching sounds. Moans like a handful of gravel being crunched under tires. I know I should get up, unlock the bedroom door and face what I have brought about, but I'm so afraid. I screwed up. Things have gone wrong and I'm horribly afraid. I know I need to face this, but I can smell her through the door.

*Oh God, Mim. What have I done?*

# TO EACH HIS OWN HELL

## *C. W. LaSart*

"Anybody else see that?" Jay pointed from the darkness of the backseat, the smoldering joint between his fingers dangerously close to Katie's long hair.

"How could we not?" Alex grabbed the joint from his best friend and took a long drag, squinting into the distance. Though fall seemed slow in coming to the Midwest, with temperatures feeling more like early June than late September, the harvest had already come and gone, leaving the fields plowed under. Visibility on country roads spread for miles in every direction. With no streetlights and only a sliver of moon, the colorful, twinkling lights up ahead had only the stars for competition.

Katie accepted the joint from Alex, wincing in distaste as the wet end touched her lips. Unable to hold the fragrant smoke for very long, hacked out a cough that caused both boys to laugh.

"What do you think it is?" The pot made her head buzz pleasantly as Katie stared at Alex's strong profile, visible only in the faint glow of the dashboard light. Reaching out to gently run her fingertips across his cheek, she squealed when he turned his head and caught one finger in his mouth with a barely perceptible wink.

"Alex!" she admonished while wiping his saliva on her skirt, though her faint, underlying laughter ruined the effect. "I said, what do you think it is?"

148

"Hell if I know. Let's drive over there and find out."

The only child of drug users, both of whom were currently in the state pen for possession and distribution of methamphetamines, Alex had been raised by his maternal grandmother. Although she'd done everything possible to give him a normal life, Alex still had a tendency to act out and cause trouble, and was a constant source of tension between Katie and her own, ultra conservative, Catholic parents. Before he picked her up that night, Katie's parents had once again rehashed that he was ruining her life because she'd opted after graduation to go to the local community college rather than accept the scholarship to the state university they'd wanted her to attend.

Katie bit her lip and watched Alex as he stared ahead at the gravel road, wondering if her parents were right. Sticking around town to be with Alex had seemed like the only natural choice, but after what they'd gone through that spring, what he'd *made* her go through, she was no longer certain he intended them to be together forever after all. Pushing aside her doubts and the unpleasant memories they dredged up, she took the offered joint from Jay and pulled the harsh smoke deep into her lungs.

*Fuck it. It is what it is.*

Alex turned left, the truck bouncing over ruts carved deep into the utility road from countless passages of some farmer's combine. The lights loomed closer, showing them what had to be a small carnival, set up in a field just off the road. A makeshift parking lot had been beaten down by the passage of vehicles, but theirs was the only one present when he pulled the truck to a stop.

"What the fuck is this?" Jay peered out from the backseat with heavy lids.

"It's a carnival, you dipshit." Alex opened his door.

"I know *that*, but what the hell is it doing way out here?" Jay pinched the lit end off of the joint and tossed the tiny roach into his mouth, grimacing as he chewed.

"I don't know." Alex said, closing the door before Jay could ask any more questions. He ran a hand across the smooth fender of his truck. The vehicle was the finest thing he'd ever owned. The only *new* thing he'd ever owned, and it never failed to fill him with an unpleasant mix of pride and guilt. His grandmother had only been dead for six months, but most of the money she'd left was already gone. This truck was the only thing he had to show for it. He'd have to get a job soon if he wanted to make the bills on the little house that he'd also inherited.

"There're no other cars. Is it even open?" Katie walked around the front of the truck to join Alex, self-consciously smoothing the wrinkles out of her short denim skirt.

"Sure it is. It's all lit up and some of the rides are running. Look," Alex pointed up and off to the right. "The Ferris wheel is going."

As if to prove his point, Katie heard a chorus of squeals and screams come from the direction of the brightly lit monstrosity that was the Ferris wheel. She shuddered, having never liked heights much, and trusted the skills of the carnies to put things together safely even less.

"So what are we doing?" Jay staggered up beside them, scratching his ass through a hole in the back of his jeans.

"I guess we're going to the carnival." Alex took Katie's hand with a wink, tugging her gently toward the bright lights ahead.

Though the sign on the ticket booth said OPEN, the little string of lights hanging around the window was off and the interior was shadowed and deserted. Alex knocked on the wooden counter and a shower of dust was the only answer.

"Maybe we should just go back to the truck. They must be closed." Katie fidgeted behind him, her sweaty hand clutching his t-shirt.

"There's no one here to sell us tickets, but there's no one here to tell us to go away, either." Alex moved to walk past the booth, stopping when neither Katie nor Jay followed. "What?"

"I don't know, man. It's kind of creepy isn't it? A carnival out in the middle of nowhere. No wonder no one's here." Jay let out a nervous laugh.

"Don't be such a pussy, Jay. Let's go check it out. The rides are running. There's got to be *someone* here. I guess we just lucked out and don't have to pay."

The three walked around the booth and were immediately swallowed up in the lively atmosphere that only a carnival could provide.

The midway assaulted their senses with bright lights, noise, and the typically overpowering, yet delightful, smell of fried food, almost strong enough to cover the odors of vomit and grease. Despite it all, Katie noticed with a growing unease the various burnt out light bulbs throughout the park and the mostly unmanned game booths. Their stuffed, Day-Glo colored prizes hung dejectedly, a snake split at the seams next to a tiger missing an eye. Both seemed to accuse her of something.

*Who'd wanna win those,* she asked herself.

They walked past a group of carnies crowded around a dart booth, but the men didn't strike up the usual banter, didn't even bother to invite them to try their luck. Alex noticed one carnie staring and gave him a nod of acknowledgement, but the swarthy man spit in the dirt and turned his back. Though the rest of them watched with suspicion as they passed, Alex didn't bother to strike up conversation. The men looked dirty, their clothing dark with sweat and grime, faces streaked with dust. Some wore filthy caps on their heads, but others had shaggy manes of oily hair that stood up in clumps. Dark eyes glittered with contempt in deeply lined and frowning faces.

Further down, a carousel spun as its poorly painted horses rose and fell unoccupied and its music strained, like a record played at the wrong speed. Someone on the Ferris wheel squealed, but it sounded more like out of terror than joy. Katie strained to hear, certain she also heard sobs coming from a ride to her left, but saw no scared or cranky child. *No one* other than the carnies.

"Alex, I want to go."

"Come on. It's a carnival. You've probably been to a ton of them and nothing bad has happened."

"I puked after riding the Tilt-o-Whirl once." Jay offered.

"I know, but it just doesn't feel right. Where is everyone? Why are they even open this late with no one here? I want to go." Katie glared at Jay.

Alex walked ahead, ignoring Katie's plea.

"Hey, look at that, babe. They have funnel cakes. Can't go to the carnival without funnel cakes." Alex grabbed her hand and pulled her toward a dingy concessions truck.

"Yeah, I could go for a funnel cake." Jay said.

The inside of the truck looked as dirty as the outside, but the enticing smell of fried food floated on the breeze and drew the three toward the window. A man stood with his hunched back toward them, the back of his head bald and liver-spotted, ringed with stringy grey hair.

"Hey buddy. How much for three funnel cakes?" Alex said, recoiling as the man turned toward his voice.

"Uh, just two." Katie put a hand over her mouth, but it did little to hide her grimace.

"Twelve bucks." His smile was more of a sneer than a friendly welcome. Teeth the color of pewter stood out at crazy angles from diseased gums, and he blinked one rheumy eye at the teens, the other a dead, white marble in his skull. A wracking cough that seemed to originate in his toes overtook him and he braced a hand on the window sill for balance, his dirty yellow nails screeching on the metal. A wave of his foul breath washed over them and Alex gagged.

"Never mind, man. You need to get yourself checked out or something."

"Fuck that. I want a funnel cake." Jay pulled some rumpled bills from his front pocket and slammed them down on the counter, his lip curling as he watched the old man scoop it up with a palsied hand.

"Dude. I wouldn't." Alex said, watching the old guy with a mixture of disgust and pity as he turned back to the fryer and squirted batter into its roiling depths. Another round of coughs shook him and he finished with a nauseating hack, spitting a gob of green snot on the floor of the truck, between his feet.

"It's fine. Shit's fried. What am I gonna catch? His hump?" Jay laughed, a hollow tittering sound that he tried to hide under a cough of his own, as the old man returned to the window and thrust a paper plate at him with a scowl.

Alex peeked at the funnel cake and had to admit, it did look pretty good. But no amount of munchies would make him eat anything that old man had touched. It would serve Jay right if he caught tuberculosis or something.

They walked down the midway, deeper into the carnival where the games of chance and rides turned into gaily colored tents with signs that promised everything from tarot readings to funhouses. The flaps were all closed and the chairs set out for ticket takers sat vacant. The empty rides droned on in the distance, their squeaking parts and warped music the only sounds in the still night.

"Aw, Christ!" Jay dropped the funnel cake into the dirt, his hand clutching his stomach as a stream of vomit hit his shoes.

"What the fuck?" Alex started, then upon seeing the problem, almost wretched himself. The funnel cake had fallen off the plate and flipped over in the dirt, revealing a mass of writhing white worms on the underside. A few tiny maggots were stuck to the plate, their eyeless heads raised in search of food. "Are those maggots?"

Jay renewed his vomiting and Katie let out a shriek as she saw it too.

"Oh man. Oh *man.* Are you okay, Jay?" She reached out to touch his arm, but Jay jerked it out of reach.

"What do you think? I just ate fucking maggots. Of course I'm not okay. I'm going to sue this place into the fucking ground. *Jesus!*" Jay swiped his mouth with the back of his hand, his lips drawn back in revulsion. His face pale, he looked like he could begin retching again at any moment.

"Let's go, Alex. Can we go now?" Katie was on the verge of tears, her complexion almost as green as Jay's.

"Oh my, this will not do. How very embarrassing." A voice, low and smooth floated out of the opening of a nearby tent. Seconds later, a slight man stepped out of the shadows, his brow furrowed in concern. "We will have to do something about this unfortunate situation. Indeed we will."

Alex had heard of people wringing their hands, but he'd never actually seen anyone do it. The small man approaching them was, his pale, spider-thin fingers worrying one another in a way that looked painful. Alex felt a bit of sympathy for the man, he seemed so bothered by the ordeal.

"Let me make this up to you, young man. I insist you allow me to make this right."

Jay wiped his hand across his mouth again, his own scowl loosening at the man's obvious concern.

"Who're you?"

"Ah yes. How very rude of me. Introductions, of course. I am Alfonso, and I run the freak show." The little man made a fancy gesture with his hand, twirling it at the wrist as he gave a deep bow.

Alex laughed at the theatrics, and saw Katie smiling out of the corner of his eye. Alfonso radiated such exaggerated gallantry, an extreme difference from the creep at the food truck. His clothing was worn, but clean, modest and neutral in shade. His long, hound dog face appeared rather pale in the dim light. What made him so humorous was the outlandish top hat upon his head, oversized and garish with a scarlet ribbon tied around the base. Alex found himself picturing the Mad Hatter in his place and was soon chuckling again. Even the dour-faced Jay grinned.

"Please, my dear young people. Allow me to grant you free passes to the freak show. To make up for this rather humiliating occurrence. You will love my show. I promise you will. Nothing like it anywhere."

"That's very kind of you," Katie said, "But I think we were leaving."

"Oh, you mustn't. Not without letting me make this up to you. Please." Alfonso was wringing his hands once again, dark eyes pleading.

"Yeah. Sure. I guess we could check it out."

"Alex! I just want to go home, okay?" Katie grabbed his hand and pulled.

"Aw, come on babe. What could it hurt? You game, Jay?"

Jay cast one last glance at the mess he'd made in the dirt and shuddered, then turned back to Alfonso, who eyed him anxiously.

"Yeah, I don't care."

"See, babe? Jay's game. If he wants to see it, I think we should go in. He *is* the one that ate the maggots." Alex laughed as Jay shot him the bird. "Let's check it out."

Alfonso clapped his hands loudly, his wide grin revealing small, evenly spaced teeth.

"You will love this." He said, drawing back the flap of a red and white tent a few feet away, beckoning them with an elaborate gesture. "Nothing like it on Earth."

Jay stepped inside and Alex pulled Katie through the opening before she could protest further. He winked at Alfonso as they passed.

"We'll be the judge of that."

"Oh yes. Indeed you will." Alfonso laughed in a pleasant way, letting the flap fall and close with a soft rustle.

The inside of the tent was dark, illuminated by several bare bulbs hung at irregular intervals. Cheap wooden walls had been erected, forming rough stalls on either side of a long aisle, each with a curtain hiding what lay inside. The trio stepped forward cautiously, their shoes scraping on the untreated wooden floor.

"Hey man, did that Alfonso guy remind you of someone?" Jay whispered, nudging Alex's arm.

"Yeah. Looked a lot like that science teacher from junior high. Mister Emerson."

"That's what I thought, but it couldn't be. Didn't he—?"

"Offed himself last year. Shotgun to the roof of the mouth I heard." Alex grimaced disingenuously. His eyes possessed a brightness born of morbid fascination.

"Yeah, that's what I heard too."

They stopped before the first stall and Alex squinted in the dim light to read what the hand-painted sign said.

"Mummy. I bet it's a fake." He pulled a cord and the curtain drew back to reveal a glass case. A spotlight hung from above, its glare shining off the glass and making it hard to see the dark figure inside. The mummy wasn't much bigger than a child, its wizened face a twisted black mask of sunken flesh and yellowed teeth. The body was also dark, the shriveled skin an oily black against decomposing bandages. Hands stiff by its sides, it had shifted forward until it rested against the glass, a gooey spot on its chest oozing dark fluid down the transparent shield.

"Eww." Katie said, clutching Alex's arm to her chest. "It looks *rotten.*"

"Dude, I don't think it's a fake." Jay sniffed the air, his mouth twisted in a grimace. "I think I can *smell* it."

"Whoever did this guy up certainly didn't do a very good job with him." Alex leaned in close to the glass for a moment, before releasing the cord and letting the curtain fall back into place. "Let's see what else he's got."

The sign on the next stall was easier to read, black letters on a white background proclaimed simply LIZARD MAN. Something behind the curtain shifted, the sound dry and unpleasant. Alex raised his eyebrows and winked at Katie, slowly pulling the cord.

"What the fuck?" Jumping back from the cage, Alex dropped the cord, but grabbed it again quickly before the heavy curtain could fall shut.

A man sat on a stool, behind the iron bars of an old-style circus cage. He was nude, but seemed unashamed as he glared back at the three onlookers, his pale eyes squinted against the light, his mouth tightened in a grim line. Nearly every inch of his skin from below the neck hid beneath crusty, grey growths, interrupted by jagged fissures that oozed yellow pus. His genitals were absurdly enlarged, encased in a solid shiny mass that only hinted at their shape, but enough to see he had what was a grotesque parody of an erection.

Katie covered her eyes. "Alex, I want to go."

"No way, babe. I've got to see the rest of this. Can you believe this shit?" Alex snickered and punched Jay in the arm, ignoring the lizard man's glare as it fell upon him.

"What do you think is wrong with him?"

"Venereal disease." Alfonso's deep voice came from behind, startling all three. Alex jumped, wondering how long he had been back there.

Stepping up close behind Jay, he laid his hand gently on the boy's arm before he continued.

"Too much time with whores and now look at that," Alfonso smiled and pointed an elegant finger at the man, his tone light and almost cheerful. "His reason for living will fall off soon. Even after he started getting bad he would go back to the whores, begging for their services, sharing his disease with anyone desperate enough to spread her legs for his coin. Sad, really. What a life he could've had if only he could control his lustful ways."

"That's awful." Katie said, turning her head from the afflicted creature behind the bars, her hand hovering nervously at her throat.

"Indeed. But many men get a taste for whores and become lost. Isn't that right, *Jay?*" Alfonso winked at the young man, his smile growing wider.

"What the fuck are you talking about? I don't fuck whores. I've never paid for it in my life!" Jay protested, his face turning red with anger and humiliation.

"That's not what I've heard." Alex joined Alfonso in laughter as Katie looked away.

"Fuck you guys." Jay said, though it came out less forceful than he intended. His right hand dropped to his crotch and unconsciously scratched. "I'm nothing like that lizard dude. That's just fucked up."

"Come on, man. I'm just screwing with you. I'm sure you're fine. Let's see what else there is in here."

Jay looked at the lizard man again, staring even after Alex released the cord and drew the curtain closed. Katie and Alex shuffled to the next stall and waited as Alfonso made one of his expansive gestures, inviting Jay to join them.

"Fuck you guys." Jay said finally, though he walked to where they stood, not looking at anyone. He scratched absently at his crotch again, and Alex raised his eyebrows at Katie, who giggled a bit despite herself.

On they went down the aisle. They passed The Fat Lady (a grotesquely large woman who Alfonso gleefully announced suffered from no apparent glandular disorder, just really loved to eat), The Wolf Man (a guy with a genetic disorder leaving him so covered in hair they could barely see his face), dwarves, a man with flippers for hands, a human pin cushion, and The Bearded Lady. All were interesting, but not terribly, in a day where such people often blended in. On they went, bored but respectful, Jay scratching his groin now and then.

"I don't mean to be rude, but how are you able to do this. Aren't their laws against exploiting people with genetic conditions?" Katie asked.

"Not if the person chooses to exploit themselves, my dear." Alfonso patted her on the arm and she pulled away slightly. "But I see my more common booths are boring you young people. Not so the next. I think you will be quite thrilled with this one."

The group stopped before yet another hand-painted sign.

"Ah yes. The Siamese Twins. May I do the honors?" Alex nodded, and Alfonso, holding the rope delicately, slowly pulled the curtains open. "My sweet little babies."

The smell was almost a physical presence, wafting between the bars and causing all three to wince. Their eyes watered as they stared in horror at the twins. The crib was large and made of iron, rust staining the thick bars. Inside lay a threadbare mattress mostly covered by filthy newspapers and a shit-caked blanket. The twins themselves lay in the center of the mess, a makeshift cloth diaper tied around their middles. Twisted pink tissue was visible just above and below the diaper line, indicating their connection at the hip and partway up the torso. They looked to be boys, and about a year old, though it was hard to tell by size, as both babies were thin and malnourished. Their dark skin, gave the impression of Middle-Eastern heritage, but some kind of illness had left their complexions ashy.

"Why?" Katie asked, tears welling in her eyes.

The infant on the left made a soft mewling cry and tried to lift his head, giving up after a brief struggle and watching the three with listless eyes. Each of his ribs stuck out, his limbs thin to the point of emaciation. Pus and thick snot leaked from his eyes and nose, while angry red streaks ran across his stomach and swirled into a spider web pattern on his sunken chest, terminating in the tissue that bound him to his sibling.

The child on the right was dead. Limbs stiff and abdomen swelling, the dead twin stared with unseeing eyes, his mouth twisted in a never ending cry. His face dark with decay, the rest of his body was mottled, marbled with blue and green corruption. Alex watched in horrified fascination as a bloated fly landed on his chin, wandered in a circle, and disappeared into his open mouth.

"What the hell?" Jay began, but before he could finish, he doubled over, unleashing a fresh torrent of vomit onto the uneven plank floor.

"Hell is subjective." Alfonso said with a smile. "Each man creates his own."

"You're a monster." Katie wept.

"Not at all, my dear. Not at all." He raised his eyebrows, his tone soft. "I found these babies in the river, just hours after their birth. Their own mother had tossed them away like trash. Deformed, unwanted. I saved them."

As Alfonso spoke, he placed a gentle hand beneath Katie's chin, pulling her face towards his own. Between the dim lighting and his ridiculous hat, she could see only his teeth and eyes, glittering in the shadows. Disturbing as his words were, she was unable to look away.

"She should have just aborted them. That would have been better for everyone, don't you think? Just a little scrape and done. Do you think the fetus feels it, Katie?"

"I…" Katie felt the world pulling away from her as she remembered.

*The smell of antiseptic. Alex wasn't there with her and she was scared.*

"I think they do feel it, don't you Katie? You do. I know you do."

*The cramps. The Doctor's cold hands. She couldn't quit crying. Not even when the nurse told her gently to "Hush." and "It will be okay. Almost done now." The pressure and scrape of tools, then nothing. Her baby, their baby. She hated Alex at that moment. Hated him with all her heart.*

"He wasn't ready to be a father." Katie sounded small, her voice weak and watery, as tears rolled down her cheeks.

"Hey man. What the fuck you doing?" Alex grabbed Alfonso by the arm and spun him around, his face twisted in rage. "What the hell do you think you're doing to her?"

Once her contact with Alfonso was broken, Katie looked at the twins once again. The barely alive child was now no longer breathing, his mouth slack. The scent of fresh shit rose from his tiny body.

"You sick son of a bitch. We're going to call the cops on you. You can't do this." Katie bit off a sob and bent at the waist as a cramp tightened her middle and a gush of warm fluid spurted from between her legs. Reaching under her skirt, she pulled out a hand slick with blood and wailed.

Jay reached out to touch Katie, then let out a shrill scream, all thoughts of her gone instantly. He saw dark and scabrous growths spreading across the back of his hand, his fingers curling into claws. He wept, alternately cradling the appendage and raking at his groin with his other hand.

"It *itches*. And my hand. Look at my hand!" Jay held his deformed digits out for Katie to see, but she was still bent over, sobbing and hugging her stomach.

"What the fuck have you done to them?" Alex grabbed Alfonso by the lapels, shaking the smaller man. "We're leaving and I'm calling the cops, man. Then I'm going to sue your ass into the ground."

Alex heard a *thwapping* noise and peered around in search of the source. There was a tear in the back wall of the tent, and a ragged flap fluttered in the breeze.

"You aren't going anywhere, son." Alfonso's tone stayed even, but he smiled just a bit. "There's only one left, and you want to see it. You *need* to see it. You can pretend to be disgusted, to be outraged, but part of you likes this."

"*Pretend?* You sick fuck!" Alex released the barker, his lips curled in disgust.

"Perhaps I am, but you are, too. Now the final curtain waits. Will you pull it, or shall I?"

"Alex, I need a doctor." Katie eyes were wild as she grabbed Alex's shirt, her hands smearing blood on it.

"We're leaving. And you can't stop us." Alex looked over at his friend who was still bawling and scratching his genitals. "Come on, Jay."

"I don't need to stop you. You're too curious. Only one left and you won't leave without seeing it. You'll wonder for the rest of your life what was behind that curtain. I don't think you'll leave."

Alex grabbed Katie's hand and made to do just that, his shoulder hitting Alfonso in the chest and shoving him aside. He made it a few feet before stopping and looking over his shoulder, his gaze falling on the closed curtain of the last booth.

*Alex!* He thought he heard his name coming from beyond the canvas.

"Alex, *please.*" Katie tugged on his hand, but still he stared at the last booth. Her blood ran faster now, down her legs and hitting the floor with dull plops.

*Alex!* It came again, and this time he was sure he'd heard it. It sounded like his grandmother's voice on the night she died.

"Just a minute, babe." Alex pulled his hand away from hers and drifted toward the sound of the voice. Katie was crying again, but he didn't notice. Alfonso smiled at the boy and nodded, pulling the rope.

A large post had been erected in the center of the cell, like an unnatural tree growing from the floorboards. Its desiccated fruit swung gently from a cross beam, twisting in the dim light. Alex took a step forward, squinting to make out the horrendous details. Eyes bulging in a face gone purple, the hanged man stared back, his protruding tongue a lump of black meat.

"What does this have to do with me? And why is he here?" Alex asked.

"He was hanged for murder. The problem is, he just won't die." Alfonso looked solemn, his glittering eyes watching Alex's face.

"What are you talking about? He's dead."

The man blinked. Alex jumped and let out a horrified yelp. The hanged man then moaned in return, his head at an awkward angle, neck broken.

"Why?" Alex found himself unable to look away from the hanged man's face no matter how hard he tried, even when Alfonso leaned in close and started whispering in his ear.

"The way I see it, you two have an awful lot in common. Both of you are murderers. Only he was dumb enough to get caught, wasn't he? I wonder what your friends would think if they really knew what happened to your dear, old granny?"

"That's crazy. I didn't kill anyone. She had a heart attack." The words sounded weak, even to him. Alex watched in fascination as the guy tried to move, his bulging eyes looking like they were about to fall out of his head. Despite his grunting, he only managed to make the rope swing a little.

"Come on, Alex. We both know that's not entirely true. She could've survived that heart attack, if you'd called the ambulance. Could've been alive today. All that woman ever did was love you and look out for you. Instead of helping her, you sat down and watched her die. You pretended to find her in the morning, but you *watched your own grandmother die.* Tell me; was this something you had thought about? Something you had planned to do if the opportunity arrived? Or was it a spontaneous decision? Was it hard to kill her?"

Alfonso smiled then, his mouth curling into a sneer.

"I didn't kill her!" Alex tore his eyes away and locked them on Alfonso.

"No. You murdered her. Murdered her by withholding help. Murder."

Alex felt his rage boil over and he struck out, punching the smaller man in the jaw and knocking Alfonso on his ass. As he fell, the top hat tumbled off, taking the back portion of his head with it. Alfonso laughed, and from where he sat in the floor, Alex saw straight through the ruined roof of his mouth, through his missing skull, and out the other side where the light glowed dully.

"It *is* Emerson." Jay mumbled with wonder, still crying softly and scoring his crotch with his ragged claw.

Katie screamed, her nails raking at her cheeks as rivulets of thick gore ran down her legs and spattered on the floor.

Alex shoved Jay towards the back of the tent, grabbing Katie around the waist and shoving her through the hole.

"You can't get away." Alfonso continued to laugh, his voice now garbled, the result of his ruined mouth. "There's nowhere to go."

Alex ignored him and pushed Jay through the hole as well, before scrambling through himself. The air outside was hot, a hellish breeze carrying the smell of burnt rubber and meat. It didn't take long to locate the source.

Many yards away, something large burned in the otherwise empty field. Alex strained his eyes against the blaze, trying to make out what it was, but Katie had already seen and she ran toward it, her high pitched keening trailing behind her. It was the truck. *His* truck. It lay on its top not far from where it had left the road, the body twisted from rolling multiple times. Thick, black smoke blanketed the sky, and the surrounding field had ignited, turning the night orange.

Jay ran toward the truck too, but tripped over something and went down hard. His mouth worked, but no sound emerged as he held up the object that had tripped him, his eyes wide with terror. The rest of his body lay a few yards away where it had come to rest after being thrown from the wreck, but he clutched his own severed head in his hands, the glassy eyes stared in disbelief.

"What the fuck?" Alex began, but stopped in awe as the head still present on Jay's shoulders slumped forward and toppled off, rolling to a stop at his feet. His body remained seated for one shocked second, before realizing it was dead and dropped to the ground.

Katie was almost to the truck now, having missed the sight of Jay's demise. In her hysteria, she ran toward it until she was too close to the fire. She stumbled to a halt just as the gas tank blew in a ball of white hot fury, incinerating her where she stood. The fireball engulfing Katie burned so brightly Alex was forced to look away. He cried out in horror, crumpling to his knees in the grass, face buried in his hands as he wept. Alex heard the crunch of grass behind him, not bothering to look up as Alfonso stopped close by.

"We're dead." He sobbed raggedly.

"I'm afraid so." Alfonso spoke sympathetically.

Alex looked up then. The fire was spreading fast, the heat nearly unbearable, but he didn't get up.

"This is hell."

"Hell is subjective." Alfonso said with a shrug. "I told you, each man creates his own."

He patted Alex on the shoulder before taking a step back from the encroaching flames.

"I have a spot for you in the show." Alfonso offered softly.

Alex thought of the freak show in the tent behind him. Saw the hanged man, the swinging rope and bloodshot eyes forced from the sockets. He heard his grandmother's voice, pleading with him. Begging him to call for help as he sat and watched.

"I would rather *burn.*"

And he *was* burning now, the flames climbing his jeans as his hair began to smolder. Alex screamed in anguish. His flesh blackened and became crispy as the world turned to unbearable suffering.

"To each his own, my boy," Alfonso said sadly and removed his hat to wipe an arm across what was left of his forehead. Watching silently, he listened to Alex's agonized cries as they mingled with the fire's roar. The shrieks rose in pitch until inhuman, becoming the chorus of all of hell and its denizens before ceasing abruptly. Alex was now nothing more than a charred lump of meat, a dark and twisted shape amidst the bright flames.

Shaking his head, Alfonso placed the hat back upon his ruined skull and turned to leave, sparing one more glance back to where what was left of Alex smoldered.

"To each his own."

# A WISE WOMAN'S REVENGE

## *C. W. LaSart*

"Do you admit your alliance with Satan, witch?"

The Magistrate leaned over the woman, spraying her face with spittle. His eyes burned with righteous fury and his face had taken on a boiled look, crimson and sweaty in the close confines of the interrogation room.

"I do not."

Elizabeth raised her chin in defiance, her voice strong despite the pain, her dignity and spirit unbroken.

"Boy, turn the crank."

The Magistrate resumed his pacing of the small room as his apprentice struggled to turn the handle on the heavy, iron crank. There was a creaking sound, though whether it was the ropes stretching or the woman's tendons, the boy knew not. She made no sound and gave no reaction other than a tightening in her face as the rack pulled her arms and legs.

Though a brutal winter storm raged outside, the temperature in the little room deep in the guts of the courthouse was stifling. A well-tended fire roared, casting its hellish glow upon the three inhabitants. A personal office for a court official originally, the room had been hastily transformed into a place for torture when the need arose. Instruments of unimaginable and unconscionable use hung from iron hooks covering the chamber walls.

"Boy! Place the pincers and brands in the fire. Be quick, now! I believe we will have need of them." The Magistrate eyed the woman spread-eagled on the rack, looking for any signs of fear or weakness brought forth by his mentioning of new tortures. Her face remained impassive, however, which only fueled his rage.

Removing his wig to blot the sweat slicking his bald pate, he took a moment to refocus, approaching his questioning from a different angle.

"Elizabeth Malloy, do you know the crimes of which you stand accused?"

"I do, Josiah."

The Magistrate flinched, narrowing his eyes at the use of his first name; the boy looked up from tending the fire, his eyes wide with shock. The accused remained obstinate, her gaze level and steady upon her tormentor.

"You will address me as *Magistrate Johnson.* I do not grant you leave to address me familiar, woman!"

"As you wish, Josiah." Elizabeth smirked at the irate Magistrate, grunting when his fist lashed out and connected with her mouth. The stone in his ring opened a stinging cut across her bottom lip. She sucked it and tasted blood, her ire piqued.

"*Miss Malloy*, you stand charged of witchcraft, a crime against our Lord. Witnesses have testified to the nature of your works. You are a sorcerer and a harlot, using your magic to infect the people of this fine town with sin. Your healings are the work of Satan and your practice as midwife nothing more than a ruse to stain the babes of this town with the mark of your master. Do you admit your treachery?"

"I admit no treachery. I have wronged no one. The citizens of this *fine* town come to my cottage when they have need of me, then they speak ill of me behind my back. Whose accusation was first, Josiah? Who cast my name into the box at the start? I think it was a jealous lover. Does this have the ring of truth?"

"Nathaniel! The crank!"

Wiry and slender at fourteen, the boy still lacked the strength and heavy muscle of manhood. He managed to make one full revolution. It was enough. Elizabeth's left shoulder pulled from the socket with an audible *pop*. She screamed once, causing Nathaniel to flinch back from the rack. As his father's apprentice for a year now, he'd witnessed dozens of interrogations, but nothing as brutal as this. It was his first witch trial.

"You don't look so sure of yourself now, woman."

Elizabeth had lost most of her color, greasy sweat running down a face pinched with pain. She moaned softly, looking away when the Magistrate pressed close enough for her to smell his foul breath. She swore to herself, when she heard they were coming for her, that she would *never* confess to their propaganda.

She planned to uphold those vows.

"Do you confess to consorting with the devil?" His tone was soft, laced with menace. "Confess and this can all be at an end."

"To hell with you, Josiah!" Elizabeth spat in his face, laughing harshly at his look of revulsion and rage. "And take this hypocritical town with you!"

The Magistrate motioned to his son to resume cranking and, though it made him feel ill at heart, Nathaniel did his father's bidding. He made as if to stop when he heard the woman's right shoulder dislocate, but his father's furious shouting spurred him on.

Elizabeth screamed, her agony echoing back from the walls of the small room as if a hundred women wailed there; nay, a thousand. The boy felt tears of sympathy roll down his cheeks.

"Confess, you witch!" Josiah shouted, throwing his significant body weight upon the woman's pelvis, forcing her hip to break with a nauseating crack that echoed like a broken branch.

Elizabeth shrieked once then fell blessedly unconscious.

Ice cold water splashed in her face, causing Elizabeth to groan and open her eyes. The pain rolled in waves, making her empty stomach spasm. Before being questioned by the Magistrate, she had sat locked in a holding cell for three days, starved the whole while in an attempt to break her spirit and sap her strength. She resorted to eating the dirty straw scattered in a thin layer across the rough wooden floor, but it cut her gums and made her vomit. She closed her eyes again and fought for sleep.

Something glowing and hot came close to her eyelid and she smelled the bitter odor of her eyebrows singeing. Elizabeth squeezed her eyes shut, praying her torment would soon be over.

"Open your eyes witch."

When she didn't comply, the scorching end of a brand pressed against her cheekbone, sizzling and smoking. She wailed and her eyes shot open, wild with pain and terror. She could see Nathaniel standing off to the side, displaying a look of genuine horror.

"Nathaniel, please!" she begged. "Make him stop. I'm innocent."

"Do not speak to my son, you wicked woman! He is too good for your wiles! You will not persuade him to do anything but the Lord's work." Magistrate Johnson punctuated his statement by pressing the burning brand to her other cheekbone. A thin stream of bile rose up her throat and threatened to choke her where she lay, unable to move more than her eyes.

"Nathaniel, hand me my knife." The Magistrate did not look at his son, merely held out his hand for the blade. Nathaniel hesitated for a second; not long, but long enough. Elizabeth's hope surfaced as she looked upon the youth with pleading eyes. He seemed unsure of what his father was doing. Perhaps she could gain his allegiance.

"Confess your sins and end your suffering."

Josiah seemed tired, the lines in his face looking deeper than they had that afternoon. His voice was steel, but his eyes seemed weary. Clearly, he thought she would have broken much sooner. Elizabeth wondered the last time *he* had eaten. Maybe he would get hungry and give up. Josiah did fancy his sustenance, among other pursuits.

"Never." Elizabeth's voice sounded more petulant now than defiant.

"So be it."

The Magistrate went about cutting off the thin shift she had been given during her imprisonment, the blade in his hand cutting flesh as well as the filthy linen barely covering her. When she lay nude and spread out on the rack, Nathaniel gasped, his wide eyes roaming the curves of her naked body. He had never in his life glimpsed what a woman looked like beneath her clothing and, though modesty demanded he look away, he could not bring himself to do it. Her sweat-slick body glowed in the fire light, painfully thin, but still possessing the maturity of a woman well into her child-bearing years.

A hard slap to the back of the head rocked him forward and tears of humiliation flooded his eyes. Nathaniel stared hard at the floor as his father berated him.

"Do not look upon the witch with lust, boy! Do you not know this is just another device she employs to bewitch your soul?" Nathaniel felt embarrassed, but a quick glance at the front of his father's robes proved he, too, was affected by the witch's nudity. Nathaniel tried to tell himself that his honorable father was above such things, that it was just his passion for the ways of the righteous inflaming him so. Still, the idea felt more hollow than comforting to the boy.

Magistrate Johnson grabbed the pinchers from the flames, holding them in such a way that Elizabeth couldn't look away from the tips, burning white at first, then red and orange. He opened them and grazed her ribs lightly, raising a blister along the tender flesh. She mewled in pain, but said nothing in retaliation.

"For the last time, Elizabeth Malloy, do you confess to the crimes of witchcraft and consorting with Satan himself?"

Hatred hardened her features against the pain. Rage seethed from her eyes, hotter than the coals in the fire that lit the room. She spoke in a low, harsh voice, her teeth gritted against the agony.

"I am no witch, Josiah Johnson! I have only healed this town's ills and delivered their young!"

"*Liar!*" he yelled, pressing the glowing ends of the pincers against her flesh repeatedly. She spoke then, her voice high and shaky with pain. "And the sins of this town outweigh my own a thousand fold! Ask the women who come to me to be rid of the babes in their bellies. Babes that do not belong to their loving, *Christian* husbands! And those same husbands who come to me with gifts to trade for my affections!"

"Shut up, whore!" The Magistrate yelled, his face so flushed Nathaniel feared he might suddenly die of apoplexy. The man poked and prodded, burning, twisting, *ripping* at her flesh, but still she screamed her words, her voice losing strength, not able to drown out the sound of sizzling meat.

"And you Josiah! Biggest hypocrite of all! Why don't *you* tell your boy the only devil I ever consorted with was you! Tell him how you came to me, lonely with the death of your wife! How I loved you with my body! This sinful body! You loved the sin, you bastard! But I didn't want you anymore, and you...couldn't...stand it!"

Magistrate Johnson dropped the pincers and leapt upon the prisoner, wrapping his meaty hands around her throat, intent on strangling the life from her. She prayed that he would, smiling through swollen lips as he lost control and squeezed harder, his face now purple and his eyes bulging with insanity. He shook her like a rag doll, slamming her head against the rack with every word.

"*YOU...LYING...DIRTY...WHORE!*"

Nathaniel jumped on his father's back, prying his hands away from the now unconscious woman's throat, holding him back until he calmed. Only when he was sure the older man no longer had murder on his mind did he let the Magistrate go.

They went out into the snowy night, the wind bitter in their faces. Nathaniel instructed the guards outside the door to untie the accused and return her to her cell. The Magistrate said nothing more. The interrogation was over for the night.

Dinner was a solemn affair, both man and boy lost in their thoughts. Nathaniel had no idea what thoughts haunted his father. He didn't really care. His own world felt shattered; the core of his beliefs shaken by the night's events. He knew that as a Christian he could not suffer a witch to live.

The Bible itself called for the execution of these "wise" women. But he couldn't shake the memory of his father's behavior, the rage driving him to nearly murder her. How could one's sins be so terrible that they deserved such punishment? And the things she had spoken, could they possibly be true? Had his father, the man he had looked up to his whole life, the one whom he modeled himself and his life after, be an adulterer? Disillusionment spoiled his usually hearty appetite.

The Magistrate ate very little and imbibed far more spirits than was prudent. The liquor itself was a sin his father hid from the world, defending his intoxication many times to his son, often telling Nathaniel *it was indeed a sin, but surely not as great as the sins of those he cast judgment upon. His job was hard, and the days were long and unpleasant. Certainly God himself could not begrudge a righteous follower some comfort at the end of his day.* Nathaniel never questioned this, following his father blindly, his future as a Magistrate secured by his birth. He wondered if he was cut out to follow in his father's footsteps.

Nathaniel had always been an obedient son, and thus what he did that night was completely out of character. He questioned his motives many times, but in the end, he just needed to *know*.

Tucking his drunken father into bed, Nathaniel kissed the old man's brow, causing his eyes to flicker open. His large hand felt weak when it grabbed the boy's wrist, his eyes moist.

"You know the whore lies, boy." The Magistrate slurred, almost immediately falling back into an uneasy slumber. He moaned but didn't awaken when Nathaniel pulled out of his grasp.

Nathaniel donned his overcoat and grabbed a lantern before heading out into the frigid night before he could lose his nerve and let good sense prevail. He clutched the long coat tightly with one hand as a fierce wind threatened to tear it off, using the flickering lantern to guide him.

Traveling all the way across town, he was nearly frozen through when he arrived. He saw no candles burning in the windows of houses he passed along the way.

Nathaniel let himself into the jail, clearly startling Thomas the guard from a deep sleep. As simple a man as Thomas was when alert, Nathaniel thought it would be easier to gain entrance at this time of night.

"What do you seek, Nathaniel?" Thomas scratched his beard, looking around confused.

"Magistrate Johnson has sent me. I have need of some answers from the accused." Nathaniel tried to place every ounce of authority he could muster into his tone.

"Can't it wait until morning? It's late and you shouldn't be here now. You understand, yes?"

"Yes, sleeping on the job. Is it not your duty to remain on guard and watch for trouble?"

"Oh, Nathaniel! I'm sorry. I know it is my duty, but—it's the witch! Yes! She must have cast a terrible spell of sleepiness upon me." Thomas' eyes darted around nervously, fearful of losing his job.

"It is alright, Thomas. Clearly, it was the work of the witch. Now if you could be so kind as to point me toward her cell...."

"Of course!" Thomas led the way, relieved to be out of trouble. He took Nathaniel to the furthest cell on the row, lighting a torch and placing it in a bracket on the wall.

The light of the flame did little to penetrate the darkness, but a shaft of cold moonlight shone through the bars of the window, bathing the back of the cell in a faint, ghostly glow. Nathaniel could just make her out as she huddled against the far wall, shivering in the dirty, straw-strewn cell. He couldn't see her face, but clearly heard the chattering of her teeth. Even in his overcoat, he felt cold when the wind whistled through the bars. She must be freezing in only her frock, without even a blanket to cover her.

"Are you awake?" He spoke softly, not wanting to wake the other prisoners.

She said something in reply in a voice too faint to hear, lost in the shrieking of the wind. Nathaniel assumed her throat must be swollen from the throttling she'd received at the hands of his father. Once again he felt sympathy rise up within for this poor woman suffering before him.

"Open the door." He motioned to Thomas, his voice firm.

"I, uh, I don't think I can do that, Nathaniel. It's against the laws and I will get into trouble."

"You will certainly be in trouble should I report your laziness. I am the Magistrate's assistant and I *order* you to unlock this cell."

"But what if the prisoner should escape?"

"This woman is in no shape to walk, let alone make an escape! If you are so worried then lock me in with her. But you better stay alert to let me out when I call."

Nathaniel leveled a glare he said seen from his father many times and, to his relief, it worked.

Though clearly unhappy with the turn of events, Thomas unlocked the door and allowed him in, then locked it again.

"Thank you, Thomas. You are a good and righteous man. Now go back to your post, the business of the Magistrate is none of your affair. This is crucial to the inquisition."

With obvious relief, Thomas retreated down the long hall, leaving Nathaniel alone with the woman who had caused him such anxiety. He began to tremble, uncertain that his idea had been wise. Now that he was here, he had no idea where to begin, and was no longer certain he could handle the truth he sought. He turned away then, his mind set on calling Thomas back from his post, when she spoke in a soft voice he again couldn't understand.

Turning back towards her, he shuffled a few feet closer, his palms slick with sweat.

"Wha-what did you say?"

Though it clearly pained her to do so, she raised her voice slightly to address him.

"I said, hello Nathaniel."

Elizabeth smiled—a ghastly sight to behold. Her eyes appeared kind, but her lips and the flesh around her mouth were swollen and discolored. Raw, red burns oozed yellow a hue from her sharp cheek bones. "I won't hurt you, boy. I couldn't even if I wanted to."

"Do you?" Nathaniel's voice was almost as quiet as hers.

"Do I what?" she looked at him quizzically.

"Want to hurt me?"

She laughed. Harsh and grating, it terminated in a bout of horrible coughing. Tears of agony coursed down her cheeks, but her eyes remained warm. "Of course not, son. Why would I want to hurt you?"

The sound of the word *son* coming from Elizabeth's mouth made Nathaniel jump. His mother had died three years prior from consumption, a nasty death stealing her from him much too soon. The boy had been close to his mother, so kind and warm was she, in contrast to his father, so stern and unemotional. He hadn't realized until that moment just how much he missed her. Something about Elizabeth reminded him of her. Maybe it was the softness to her eyes, the sadness of her smile. Her hair had been shorn by a group of righteous women in search of the devil's mark. He wondered if it had been a rich auburn color like his mother's hair.

Suddenly, Nathaniel felt more alone in the world than he ever had before in his life. Bitter tears began to run down his face and he did nothing to stop them.

"My father, the Magistrate. He...he did *this* to you!" Nathaniel motioned with his hand, the gesture encompassing her ruined body. "You must hate me for being his son."

"Don't be silly, boy. I do not hate you. You are not responsible for the sins of your father, no matter what the church may teach you, no matter what any man says to doubt you."

The wind gusted again, causing her body to be wracked with chills. She winced and Nathaniel moved, unsure of what he planned to do until he was doing it.

He shrugged out of his heavy coat and placed it gently upon her. It still bore his youthful warmth, and Elizabeth sighed with relief, brushing a gentle kiss across his brow when he leaned across her to tuck the edges in. Nathaniel froze stunned by the longing her simple gesture filled him with. He felt not only embarrassed by her gratitude but was most uncertain about his father's actions.

"Thank you, Nathaniel." Elizabeth whispered then, recognizing his discomfort, changed the subject. "Ask your questions."

"My questions?"

"Surely you didn't come here just to offer your father's prisoner your coat after your long journey in the cold?"

"No. I guess not." He fidgeted and looked at the wall, suddenly unsure about questioning her. "I just have one question, really."

"You want to know if I spoke the truth? I know you don't want to hear this, but, yes, I spoke the truth."

Nathaniel pulled away from her, filled with a cold rage. His fists clenched and he suddenly wanted nothing more than to snatch his coat back and leave.

Before he did, maybe he would punish her *himself.* Make her pay for the doubt she had cast into his life. She gazed calmly at him as confusion overwhelmed him with anxiety.

"*YOU LIE!*" Nathaniel screamed, reverting into his father.

"I have no reason to lie, Nathaniel." Her tone remained even, though it clearly pained her to speak this much.

"You have *EVERY* reason to lie!" He didn't want to believe her, *couldn't* believe her. If she was telling the truth, then everything he knew, everything he stood for was wrong.

"What reason do I have to lie? What have I left to defend? I was guilty before charged in the eyes of this town and the eyes of Josiah Johnson, Honorable Magistrate. They will kill me whether I confess or not. I am a dead woman. *He* has every reason to lie. He stands to lose *you, Nathaniel. YOU!*"

Her words were harsh, yet there was no bitterness laced her tone, only a sad and tired acceptance. Nathaniel's rage began to cool, and as he looked into her serene eyes as shame flooded in, replacing his anger. He was no better than his father.

"Do you know what my sin is, Nathaniel?"

"Yes," he replied weakly, looking at the filthy hay-strewn floor. "You are accused of witchcraft and being in league with the devil."

"No, son. That is not my sin. My sin is simply being different. Not believing in the same things they do. Not allowing myself to be dominated by man."

Nathaniel looked up astounded, the impact of her words hitting him harder than any physical blow. Looking into her wise eyes as she spoke, he recognized this wisdom as truth.

"Did you know that I was married once?" Elizabeth looked at Nathaniel squarely, continuing on when he didn't respond. "He was a wonderful man and I loved him more than anything. We didn't have long together. He was killed fighting another man's war and I miss him to this day. The rules of society said I needed to remarry. At my age I could still provide children for another man. I refused. I became an outcast and moved to the woods to make my life in nature."

She shrugged, winced at the pain this brought, and smiled thinly. Nathaniel liked the sound of her voice. She seemed so kind and wonderful. He felt a deep bond forming within his heart for her.

"You see son, religion is a powerful thing. It has the power to lift men up and show them greatness, but it also has the power to destroy men. To corrupt them. Any power is dangerous. This religion has become a hard thing. It can turn a good man murderous. You've seen what it has done to your father. This Jesus that the bible talks about, He was all about love, wasn't He?"

Nathaniel nodded, hating where she was going with this, but still following her words nonetheless.

"Tell me, Nathaniel. Do you believe Jesus would condone this sort of behavior? Jesus, who loved all and forgave all according to the Good Book? Would He allow, were He here today, the things your own father has done?"

Nathaniel trembled. Her words made sense and he knew he believed her. The foundations of his faith began to crumble. All he had ever been taught came into question. His father, the man whom he had held in the highest regard, now loomed in his mind as flawed and corrupt.

"What will I do? How can I become a Magistrate after this? How can I go home now and face the monster my father has become?" Nathaniel implored, his large eyes overflowing with grief.

"Who says you have to do those things?" She asked gently.

"I have no choice in the matter! As the Magistrate's son, I am bound to follow him."

Elizabeth shook her head. "By following the rules of men you are. Can you not make your own rules as I have?"

Nathaniel felt stunned. The concept of making his own choices had never occurred to him. Suddenly he was as sure of this woman's innocence as he was of his mother's goodness. He had to help her.

Nathaniel jumped to his feet and began to pace the cell.

"We have to get you out of here! I will call the guard. I will disable him in some way…"

"Wait."

Nathaniel turned at the conviction in her voice.

"I'm dying, Nathaniel. The sun has set on me for the last time."

Panic welled in his chest. He had just found this woman, this Elizabeth, who had just torn the wool of lies and injustice from his eyes, and he loved her for it.

"There is something you can do for me, though." Elizabeth said her fate clear in her eyes.

"Anything."

"When I knew they were coming for me, I secreted on my person a vial of poison. Before I was questioned, I slipped it into the large crack in the floor over there. I can't move anymore, son. Will you retrieve it for me?"

Nathaniel froze, uncertain as to whether he should comply with her last wish.

"*Please, Nathaniel!* Let me die on my terms, not at their hands. I'm already close to death."

Nathaniel pushed his feelings about taking one's own life aside and strode across the cell to kneel down and reach into the crack. It was dark and he felt fuzzy things that made his mind recoil in horror, but located the small glass vial. It contained a dark, murky fluid. He wondered if it smelled bad. *Like death.*

He returned to her side.

"Is there enough?" he eyed the small vial dubiously.

"More than enough." She smiled at him gratefully. "I need you to pour it in my mouth. I can hold nothing now."

His heart thundering in his chest, Nathaniel opened the poison and began to pour it into her mouth. On impulse, he stopped when it was half gone, threw his head back, and swallowed the remaining contents. The fluid tasted bitter, but felt warm in his throat.

Elizabeth wept. There was no use for words. She knew why he had done it, but nothing in this life could be taken back. There were only amends. Nathaniel wrapped his arms around her, careful not to put any pressure on her injuries. They lay quietly for a long time with nothing but each other's breathing for comfort. As Elizabeth drifted off, a thought occurred to her. Without intending to, she had exacted a sort of revenge on the Magistrate. When he finds his only son there in the morning, sharing the embrace of death with his former lover, his grief will be unimaginable.

The thought brought her no comfort in the least.

As the darkness of death came for them, Elizabeth once again danced with her husband, secure in his arms as he twirled her around the dance hall on the night they first met.

Nathaniel dreamed of his mother.

# SIRENS

## *C. W. LaSart*

"Peder! Get back from the bow and man your oars before the sea witches drag you to your death!" Zeth scowled at his sister's only son, where he sat perched on the edge of the boat, his oar left dragging through the blue water. By fourteen summers, Zeth had thought the boy ought to be ready to begin his training as a fisherman, but now he was beginning to wonder if bringing Peder along had been a mistake. The boy seemed soft, not tough enough for the rigors of life at sea. The boy seemed to embrace the doctrines of the new priests, and Zeth had wondered for a time whether Peder might be better suited to a life in the clergy, but Zeth had cast away the thought. Peder was entirely too interested in dalliances with the fairer sex, like his father had been before him. Zeth sighed. His brother-in-law, Cadmus, had been an excellent seaman in spite of his love of the ladies, so perhaps there was hope for Peder.

"You've been spoken to, boy! Mind your elders!" Otis barked. His voice was a rough sound that matched his weathered features and scraggly beard. He looked much older than his 40 years. Too much sun and the harsh, salty spray etched premature lines in the face, often making a man of middle years appear ancient. When Peder didn't take up the oar, Otis slapped him upside the head. The young man scowled but grabbed the oar and began to row in time with the others. Although

188

their boat was large enough for eight men, the village could only spare four at a time.

"Tell me more tales about the sirens, Zeth." Peder's eyes gleamed with mischief. "Will they have fish tails?"

Otis answered before Zeth could, rolling his eyes and grumbling. "Don't be a fool boy. Mers have the fish tails. Sirens are the ones with wings. Merfolk are nothing compared to Sirens."

"Like angels' wings?" The boy's smile was mocking.

Zeth sat back, aghast at Peder's lack of knowledge about the sea's dangers. Though their island had been converted to Christianity many years before, the older ones understood that accepting Christ did not mean the old stories held no truth. No matter how much a man tried to adhere to the teachings of the Church, they could not erase from their minds the things they'd seen. The young seemed to believe everything the missionaries taught on Sundays, but the ones who had lived enough summers had learned to form an alliance between old ways and new beliefs. Zeth believed in the Savior, Christ, but he also knew there were things that the Church refused to acknowledge, that ancient monsters still lived that were no longer supposed to exist in the new world.

"You guys really believe those legends?" Peder laughed. "You know that's blasphemy don't you?"

Otis shook a gnarled fist at the boy, his ire piqued by Peder's patronizing tone. "You of all people shouldn't be so quick to disregard the traditions of the old ones! You'll see. This time it might be *you* drained and drug off to your death instead of your--"

"Otis!" Zeth warned, and the other man quieted instantly, embarrassment coloring his cheeks. Otis looked away; squinting out at the sea with more intensity than was warranted. Peder looked from Zeth to Otis, his eyes narrowed, certain there was a secret being kept from him.

"What? What was Otis going to say?"

"Nothing, son. Nothing." Zeth raised a stern eyebrow to Otis, who reluctantly nodded his agreement without looking Peder in the eye.

"Wasn't gonna say nothing, boy, except you shouldn't be so quick to insult men who have seen more years than you. Now mind your rowing." Otis left no room for further conversation. The four men continued to row as a team, staying close to the shoreline, as the fourth man, Theon, began to sing a soft melody about the sea. Theon was younger than the other two men, his children not yet grown. His voice was fine and strong, lulling the others into a quiet companionship.

Zeth wondered if he shouldn't tell Peder what had truly happened while the boy was still clutching his mother's skirts and soiling his britches. Maybe if Peder knew what had become of his father, Cadmus, he might take their warnings seriously. But then again, there was no guarantee that Peder would believe them; having been told for so many years that Cadmus had drowned in a fishing accident. The only souls who knew the truth were the three in this boat, and that was how they had agreed it would stay. Zeth knew that his sister, Naia, had her suspicions, but she had suffered so much with his infidelities in their short marriage, that none of the men could bear to affirm that Cadmus had been lured to his death by a beautiful Siren. The knowledge would only add agony to her injured heart. The temptation to tell Peder the truth passed once again. Zeth's own wife had died giving birth to their third daughter, leaving Zeth sonless. He realized that, as Naia's brother, the responsibility of teaching his nephew the ways of manhood should fall to him, but by God, Peder was so damn smug and irritating! Zeth couldn't fault Otis the desire to throw the cocky boy overboard. If only his father hadn't died when he was so young. Growing up with only a mother had done little to toughen the boy. He was a spoiled and pampered whelp. Zeth sighed.

The boy wouldn't let the older men's silence rule. "Tell me Theon, do you also believe this blasphemy talk of sea witches and monsters?" Peder's eyes gleamed with mischief already.

"I believe my own eyes. I know what I have seen." Theon nodded gravely. "Perhaps it's not blasphemy. Have you considered that the monsters of lore might be the demons the priests warn us about, sent to tempt our souls to sin?" He shrugged and continued rowing, his eyes fixed on the coastline. A cool breeze had begun to blow, the sun descending toward the horizon. They would soon be traveling in the dark. "Pick up your pace, men," Zeth said. "We want to be beyond the channel before twilight leaves us." Theon agreed, Otis nodded and, for once, Peder remained silent.

The cliffs rose up on each side, dark jagged spikes that filled the air with spray where the water crashed against rocks. The sea became rougher, pushing the vessel this way and that as the men struggled with the oars. The daylight was fading fast and twilight gave the world a faint purple cast, reflecting off the mist.

Peder manned his oars, but that didn't stop the young man from running his mouth, taunting his uncle every few moments.

"So what will your sea witches do with me if they catch me?" he called to Zeth's broad back as the older man struggled with the current.

Zeth sighed and glanced over his shoulder at the smiling youth. Raising his voice to be heard over the pounding waves, he responded. "They will beguile you, then drain you of your life's blood and leave your lifeless body broken upon the rocks."

"But these are sea hags! How can such a being *beguile* me? Ha ha! I only love the finest women. And how will they get my blood? I think you old men have spent too much time in the sun to believe this nonsense. Perhaps your brains have been cooked soft! And if you are so afeared of these creatures, why do you even brave the channel at all? Why not just go around it?"

"You ask too many damn questions!" Otis scowled. "You well know to skirt the channel we would lose a whole day's fishing! You shouldn't mock—"

"Calm yourself, Otis," Zeth said gently. "Let's tell the boy what he needs to know. Perhaps we will be lucky enough to avoid the Sirens and he can go on thinking us addled old fools."

Peder, clearly amused by the exchange, leaned into his oar with an easy rhythm as he waited to hear his uncle's explanation. Zeth gathered his thoughts for a moment before he started, talking loudly and looking over his shoulder to ensure the boy was taking it all in. They were well into the channel now and the time for talking would soon be at an end.

"When the time comes, you must look at the water. Help us avoid the rocks, but do not look up, no matter what you *think* you see. Looking at them is bad; they get into your head through your eyes. So if you do see one, look away fast. You will feel you must look, and you will. We all did the first time, but you must tear your eyes away from them as soon as you can. There is power in beholding them, but hearing them is the most dangerous thing. That is why I gave you the wax plugs. Soon it will be time to put them in your ears. They won't block out the sounds completely, but the effect of siren song will be muted. Without the wax in your ears, you could not resist the lure of their singing."

"What do they sound like?" Peder asked with awe, unsure whether it was the gravity of his uncle's voice that made him want to believe, or just the power of the tale.

"Angels." Theon said softly beside him. His rugged face looked haunted. "Angels that will drink your blood through any orifice they can find."

Though Theon remained grave, Peder burst out laughing at the statement, his adolescent humor overcoming the solemn atmosphere and earning a scowl from even his good-natured ally.

"I told you it was a mistake to take this whelp with us!" Otis complained to Zeth. "Damn fool can't take anything serious. He's not even old enough to grow hair on his stones!"

"There's enough hair on my stones to please your Hallie on cold nights!" Peder responded, his shot hitting Otis in a sore spot. The older man swung a fist, but Peder ducked, laughing. Theon fought hard to keep his own face neutral, but it was a losing battle. His shoulders shook with restrained mirth as he tried to calm Otis and get him back to his own rowing. Hallie was Otis' youngest daughter, and the whole village knew she had a soft spot for the young men of the village, and that many had received their first instruction in the art of physical love at her expert hands

"Stop it, you fools!" Zeth held up a warning hand, his head cocked to the side like an old, weathered hound. "Do you hear it?"

Peder and the rest quit rowing, leaving the boat to rock unsteadily as waves hit it from both sides. He strained hard, at first hearing nothing but the water lapping at rocks. Then something else joined the surf, soft and subtle, almost a phantom of a sound, though growing steadily louder with each passing moment. It was singing. Girls singing. Peder's jaw dropped.

"Damn!" Zeth exclaimed as he fumbled in his pocket for the wax plugs. "Put them in *NOW!*"

Peder reached into his own pocket, panicking as he searched, finally coming up with the hard wax his uncle had fashioned for him before they had left that morning. Excitement and fear warred within his chest as he allowed himself to wonder whether the stories might be true. Were there really such things as Sirens? He knew, at least, that the worried men around him believed in them with all their hearts. What about the rest of the fairy tales mothers told small children in their beds? Could they all be true? He opened his mouth to ask, but the other three men had bent over the oars, heads down and ears plugged. He glanced at Theon and was shocked to see that his big, brave friend looked near tears with anxiety. A thrill of terror ran through him. *What fearsome hags these sea witches must be!*

The ethereal voices grew in volume until Peder felt the singing must surely originate in his own head. Peder had never heard anything so beautiful, so heart-

194

wrenching that tears flooded his eyes. The tune was wordless but magnificent. Nothing of this earth could sound so sweet, piercing his mind like golden rays of sunshine. He was astonished to feel the first stirrings of an erection, the song of the Sirens entering his ears and traveling his entire body to tug pleasantly at his groin. His whole body vibrated with the pure sounds. He gasped aloud, an involuntary *"AH!"* of pleasure.

Unable to resist, Peder looked up from the water, squinting his eyes in the gloom to catch sight of the ancient myths that produced such wondrous song. Scanning the edge of the cliffs, his breath caught in his throat as the first siren came into view. She burst from the mist where water met rock, shooting high and fast, spiraling into the air with her wings wrapped tightly around her body. As she began to fall, she opened those lovely, diaphanous wings and floated gently back down, the sound of her laughter like bells in his feverish brain. Two more erupted from the spray, beautiful and pale where they drifted on the breeze, their merry song echoing off the rocks. The first fluttered like a butterfly, slowly gliding towards Peder where he stood on the rocking boat, oar forgotten in his numb hands.

How could anyone ever describe such magnificent beings as witches or hags? Surely, the Angels themselves in Heaven couldn't be lovelier! Peder stared in stunned awe as the siren floated mere feet away from him; certain he would never see such beauty again. Her wings were large and translucent, gently veined in blue like the finest silk from the Orient. Her eyes were nearly colorless in a face finer than those of the ancient goddesses no longer worshipped by his people. Her body was that of a girl, only recently crossing the threshold of womanhood.

Small, perfect breasts and long coltish legs, her waist narrow and the juncture of her sex smooth and hairless, her whole body a pale shade of blue, marbled by darker veins. She smiled at Peder and beckoned with slender hands, drifting close enough to touch.

Zeth shouted a warning and swung his oar at the creature, trying to break the spell that held Peder tightly, but another of the sirens darted in and grabbed the end of the oar, beginning a ferocious game of tug of war with him that required help from Otis. Theon himself was busy batting at the other sea witch, as she also tried to steal an oar, intending to leave them stranded and at the water's mercy. Peder stood paralyzed, his own oar sliding from his hands to be swallowed by the sea.

The siren landed weightlessly on the boat beside Peder. She was taller than he was, but so very slender and feminine. He reached out to her, shuddering with ecstasy as his hand clasped the firm, cold flesh of her breast. She smiled and reached up to cup his cheek gently, her slender fingers deftly pulling the plug of wax from his ear as he rolled her frigid nipple between his fingers. He rocked back slightly under the full assault of her voice singing that sweet wordless tune, though her mouth never moved. She gathered him up in her arms, his warmth against her chill, and her strong wings carried them aloft on the breeze.

"*NO!*" Zeth screamed as the sea witch snatched his sister's son into the air. Giving his opponent one final thrust with the oar, he broke free and ran to Peder's empty side of the boat. Falling to his knees, he cried out the boy's name as the sea pushed the vessel towards the sharp rocks lining the channel.

196

"Zeth! The rocks!" Otis yelled, using his oar to push off time and again, as they were nearly battered against the cliff walls. The siren that had been plaguing Theon had given up as soon as Peder was carried up into the air. Theon too, struggled to keep them from being wrecked against stone. But Zeth ignored them both, staring in agony at the sky where his nephew drifted, held in the embrace of a beautiful monster.

Peder felt no fear, enraptured by the siren; he tipped his head back to accept her cold kiss. He tasted the salt of the sea on her blue lips as he opened his mouth wide to her. He offered no resistance as her long tongue unfurled like the proboscis of a butterfly, darting down his throat to pierce his heart, an unholy straw. Peder gurgled as she drank, his face frozen in shock as his persistent young heart continued to pump, giving away his lifeblood with every beat.

The second Siren tore at his britches with claw-like hands, shredding them away until she was able to bury her face between pale buttocks, her own tongue diving deep to find a vessel from which to feed. The third flew around aimlessly for a moment before deciding that his exposed ear was best for a meal. Zeth watched it all helplessly, his sobs echoing back from the rocky cliffs as the monsters drained Peder dry.

Zeth nearly threw himself into the sea with anguish. He had failed his sister, once again! Theon held him back.

There was no pain for Peder, only an overwhelming bliss in which he found climax, spurting what small amount of fluid he had left against the hard, cold stomach of his deadly mistress. When the Sirens had fed, they released him, his body plummeting into the waves below, where it floated face up for a moment before turning in the surf and submerging in the depths. Theon moved to go after him but this time it was Zeth who did the restraining.

"He's gone," Zeth said softly, as Theon struggled to be free.

"But his body! I must take him home to his mother!"

"It's too late, Theon."

Sated on young Peder's blood, the sirens flew off into the darkness, their laughter ugly and harsh compared to their previous joyous song. Zeth watched them disappear as he sat heavily on the bottom of the boat. The waters were already calming as they drifted out of the channel toward the fertile fishing waters.

"We will tell her he drowned. It will be easier that way," said Zeth.

Zeth's head hung low, his spirit defeated. Large, salty tears coursed down his cheeks to mix with the spray coating his weathered face. Silent sobs wracked his body as Theon embraced the older man.

"Damn young fool!" Otis spat into the sea, but his eyes were red and moist with grief.

The fishing boat drifted slowly out of the channel and the three men discussed what story they would deliver to a heartbroken mother. Unbeknownst to them, something watched from deep within the rock's shadows. Eyes the depthless black of a shark's, stared, unblinking, until they were out of sight. Teeth like needles clicked open and shut in metallic anticipation of the meal to come.

The mermaid slid silently into the water, propelled by her powerful tail to Peder's final resting place on the sandy bottom of the sea. Tender tidbits such as the eyes and testicles would be devoured first, and she wanted to get them before the fish did.

# MOMMY

## *C. W. LaSart*

The noises started during dinner; faint at first, then they grew loud enough that Emma could no longer ignore them. They were whistling sounds, like the one a draft through a cracked window makes when the wind hits it just right. It was like a storm that only Emma could hear. She laid her fork on her plate and looked at the ceiling, her eyes wide and unfocused.

Her brother, Daniel, stared at her with his fork hovering halfway to his open mouth. A dollop of gravy fell onto his shirt, while Grams' eyes went wild, scanning every inch of the room. Only Mommy continued to eat her dinner, her attention to her plate, unwavering.

Finally, Mommy asked softly, still not looking up. "Are they coming?"

Emma shrugged her shoulders. "Maybe not this time."

Mommy looked up at Emma. There was no anger in her grim, grey face, only a hardness that served as a warning to her young daughter against lying.

Emma dropped her own gaze back to the table, shoulders slumped in defeat. "Yes, Mommy. They're coming."

"The good ones... or the bad ones?" Mommy asked. She sounded tired, as if the answer didn't matter either way. The others at the table held their breath,

"The bad ones."

Grams moaned and Daniel put his head in his hands.
"When?"

"Soon. Tonight, maybe."

"Who?"

"I don't know."

"Try, baby," said Mommy. "You have to try. So we can be ready."

Emma squinted her eyes and screwed up her little face in concentration, staring hard at a spot high up on the wall. She rocked lightly in her seat, her frail body seeming to draw in on itself as she did so. Everyone waited. No one spoke or even moved until Emma stopped and looked at Mommy with big blue eyes welling with tears.

"Who?" Mommy was firm but gentle.

Emma's small hand pointed to the floor where a young hound dog lay snoozing. "Daisy."

The little girl choked back a sob, causing the dog to crack one sleepy eye in concern, but after determining that no one was going to drop her a tasty treat, the dog drifted back to sleep.

Mommy nodded before returning her attention to her plate. "Finish your dinner."

The four of them gathered in the living room. Grams sat in her favorite rocking chair, her eyes focused on the fireplace, lost in her own haunting memories. Daniel and Emma curled up together on the couch, their attention moving from Mommy, who sat in the armchair reading aloud from a book of bedtime stories, then to Daisy asleep on the floor, then back to Mommy. Daddy's pistol lay on the end table within easy reach of Mommy. The air in the room seemed to crackle with anticipation.

Emma had been able to see and hear the shadow people for as long as she could remember. She didn't know why she was the only one, but in her ten years, she had never met another person who could. She still prayed to God every night that the shadows would go away and leave her alone, but they never did. Sometimes they would stay away from her for weeks or months at a time, but just when she started to let hope creep in that they were gone for good, they always returned.

Some of them weren't so bad, though they caused a lot of mischief, breaking things and pulling pranks. She called these shadows the *good ones*. They never really harmed anyone. Light like a wisp of smoke, their whispers sounded airy and playful. Thick and dark, the *bad ones* oozed around like oil, their voices gravelly and harsh. When *the bad ones* showed up, someone always died.

Emma could see them now, oozing around the little dog, asleep before the fire. Daisy breathed a deep sigh, drawing the darkness in through her nostrils.

"Mommy!" Emma interrupted her mother's story.

Everyone in the room looked up and froze, except Mommy. Without taking her eyes off the dog, she picked the gun up from the table. She pulled the hammer back silently and aimed.

Still asleep, Daisy growled then her eyes snapped open. The rumbling in her chest sounded so loud in the now silent room, and the short hair on the dog's back and shoulders stood on end as she bared her teeth in a feral grin. Gone was the family pet. Reflected flames from the fireplace glowed in her crazy eyes. Daisy glared at the pistol in Mommy's hand. The nervous tension in the

202

room felt palpable and even Mommy held her breath, waiting for the beast to move.

Grams broke the stalemate, accidentally dropping her needlepoint hoop to the floor. When the dog lunged forward to snap at the old woman, the blast of Daddy's pistol made an impossibly *huge* noise in the small room. Gore splattered the hem of Grams' housecoat, as the upper portion of Daisy's skull was exploded. The dog dropped with a thud, dead on the floor before them.

It was over.

For now.

Emma shrieked and ran to Grams, scrambling onto her lap and curling into a ball. Grams held her while she wept; rocking the child and whispering soothing words, her own wrinkled cheeks wet with tears. Mommy sat still as stone in her chair, her eyes locked on what was left of the dog. Her shaking hands, still gripping the gun, were all that revealed how affected she was by the experience.

Daniel paced the room anxiously, his hands balled into fists at his sides, adolescent rage causing color high on his cheekbones.

"*JESUS! Why does this keep happening?* Why do we keep getting dogs? Why do we even bother?" Daniel's voice cracked at the end, and to everyone's astonishment, especially his own, he burst into tears.

Only Mommy remained stoic. She hadn't shown much emotion for a long time. Not since what had happened with Daddy and Amber. She worked hard to protect them all from the shadow people, but could offer little else in the way of human comfort. Mommy didn't look up from the dog when she spoke.

"You know why, Daniel. It's because they like to take the dogs, and it's better they take a dog than one of us." With that, she stood and put the gun back in the cabinet drawer, before walking slowly to the bathroom where they kept the cleaning supplies.

Daniel watched her go, shaking his head and speaking low under his breath. "Maybe we should get smaller dogs."

When Emma first started talking about the shadow people, her parents thought they were harmless invisible friends, created in the active imagination of their five-year-old. At first only the *good ones* came. Things started happening; dishes falling off counters when no one stood nearby, cupboard doors opening and closing by themselves, things going missing. Mommy and Daddy became uneasy and concerned, but tried their best to ignore it. After all, no one ever truly got hurt, other than the occasional shallow cut, like the one Daniel received while he was picking glass out of a window that one of the things had slammed shut.

It was Amber, Emma's older sister and her favorite person in the world, who first suggested the shadow people might be poltergeists. She did research in the library. Poltergeists, she claimed, often attached themselves to a young child, only leaving when the kid grew too old to hold their interest anymore. Mommy and Daddy hadn't wanted to believe this at first. They considered themselves too rational and intelligent to subscribe to such ideas. But as time went by and the phenomena occurred more frequently, they could no longer deny that something was happening. So they told no one else, sold the house and moved their family to another town.

But the shadow people moved with them.

Shortly after they had settled in the new house, the *bad ones* made their first visit. Emma was scared of the *bad ones,* she tried to explain to Mommy how they were *different* than the others, but even after all they had been through, Mommy didn't quite believe her. She had rocked her sobbing daughter, trying to comfort her with silly songs that eventually stopped the tears and brought a smile to her child's chubby face. When she tucked Emma into bed, the little girl had clutched her hand tightly and whispered in a small, fearful voice.

"It's Mr. Jeffreys, Mom. Mr. Jeffreys next door."

"What about him, honey?"

"I think he's gonna hurt Mrs. Jeffreys. Real bad. Like dead."

Mommy froze for a moment, her blood feeling cold in her veins. She mustered up a smile for her daughter, whom she loved so much. "It's okay, honey. I'm sure that won't happen. Mr. Jeffreys is a nice man and he loves his wife a lot. He won't hurt her." She hoped the doubt in her heart wasn't evident in her voice.

After Mommy tucked Emma in and turned out the light, she went to the room down the hall that she and Daddy shared. She closed the door behind her and did something she hadn't done since childhood. She dropped to her knees by the bed and prayed. *God,* she prayed aloud in a soft voice, *please save my family from the evil that has befallen us, and please protect my baby Emma from this burden upon her shoulders.*

In the middle of the night, Mommy and Daddy woke up to the sound of a woman screaming next door. Mommy called the police, while Daddy dressed and ran next door to help, but he was too late. Mr. Jeffreys stood on his front step with stooped shoulders and a vacant expression, wearing nothing but bloodied boxer shorts. In his clenched right fist, he held a wickedly long kitchen knife, red with gore. When the police showed up, they demanded he *drop the knife!* He refused, advancing on them instead, his weapon raised high. They shot him dead on his own front yard. Mommy knew then, but didn't dare admit it—the *bad ones* had taken their first lives.

Daddy insisted that the family move again. And once again, the shadow people followed them. Life in their home changed drastically once the *bad ones* had come. Daddy drank more, which caused fights with Mommy. Daniel became angry, lashing out at everyone. Emma became withdrawn. Only Amber remained cheerful, often hugging Emma and playing with her.

Amber would tell her the troubles weren't her fault; she was just *special*, but Emma knew differently. She knew she was the reason the shadow people came. Daniel told her so, every time they were alone. He had always teased and picked on her in the past, but this was different. He *blamed* her.

There seemed to be no rhyme or reason to the visits by the spectral trespassers. Amber spent months trying to track them, questioning the sullen Emma and writing notes about every supernatural event that happened. Sometimes, for months, only the good ones would wreck their havoc. Then, nothing at all would happen, for weeks. The bad ones would come, sometimes once every few months, then suddenly, several times in the space of a few days. Amber finally gave up, learning nothing from her chart's chaotic lines and numbers.

The bad ones mostly went after their dogs. The first time it happened was the hardest. The lab mix, Buster, had been their beloved pet for years. After Buster died, the family made a point to keep their emotional distance from the animals. Except Emma, of course. At only nine years old, it was impossible for her not to fall in love with every new dog. Also, as no one in the family dared develop close friendships for fear the shadow people might target them pet dogs were all Emma had. Even though Mommy urged her to try not to become attached, Emma continued to give the dogs names. Every time the bad ones took another dog from them, her little heart felt torn from her chest.

Emma knew it was wrong to think so, but she came to prefer the rare times when the bad ones took a person, instead of an animal. The shadow people had only taken distant neighbors or people she only knew vaguely. Once, it had been Daniel's teacher, a stern woman he didn't like, anyway. Daniel was actually especially nice to Emma for a while after that one, as if she had any control over who the shadow people chose.

By the time Emma announced their fifth dog, Bugs, as the next target, they'd all become somewhat accustomed to what these announcements brought. It was Daddy's idea to put the dog down *before* it became possessed, or whatever it was the shadow people did to make it go crazy. Mommy hadn't liked the idea from the start, but when Daddy drank, he could be very persuasive. The three children sat by and listened as he explained to Mommy that he was afraid the dog might attack one of them tonight before he had a chance to shoot it. Mommy finally gave in to Daddy's argument, and after tearful goodbyes from the children, he took the docile mutt away. He came back alone and visibly shaken. He had discovered that it is a lot harder to shoot a family pet *before* it turned on you. They all soon retired to bed. Emma thought about Bugs for a long time and then cried herself to sleep.

Emma didn't actually see what happened that night between Daddy and Amber, but she heard a lot of things she wished she hadn't. When the screaming started, she hid under her bed, pressing her small fingers into her ears to block out the sounds. She didn't know what was going on, but she could tell it was coming from Amber's room. She wanted desperately to run in there and protect her big sister, but in the end, she was just too scared.

Mommy's screams picked up where Amber's trailed off. Daddy never said a word. Emma heard the gunshots. *One...Two...Three...* then a crashing sound as Daddy hit the floor. Mommy sobbed loudly for a moment, before Emma heard her muffled voice speaking into the phone.

Just before the police arrived, Mommy gathered Daniel and Emma together and brought them downstairs to the living room. The next two hours were a blur of policemen in blue and coroners in white. Questions were asked while flashes of light erupted from the upstairs hall as the scene was meticulously photographed. Before they interviewed Mommy, she asked that they move to the kitchen. She didn't want *the children to hear,* but they already knew the worst. The shadow people had come for Daddy, and he had killed Amber.

Daniel had glimpsed Amber's room. He whispered to Emma, telling her what he had seen there. She didn't want to hear it, but listened anyway, too shocked and exhausted to stop him. Daniel told her about the blood.

There had been so much of it that it was even on the ceiling. He said that Daddy was naked, and that his hands were all bloody. Daniel said he thought he had done it with just *his hands*, and Emma yelled at him to *SHUT UP!* , earning a look from a nearby investigator.

They moved again, and this time, Grams came to live with them. Grams was Mommy's mother, and they all adored her. She hadn't known about the shadow people before, but now Mommy had no choice but to tell her. Grams stayed to help Mommy protect the children, but she didn't deal well with the supernatural occurrences that centered around her youngest granddaughter. Not being used to these episodes, she was very afraid of the *good ones*.

Despite living in a constant state of apprehension, Grams did her best to help the children's lives return to some semblance of normal. She cooked and cleaned, praised Daniel and Emma over their schoolwork, and comforted them in moments when their grief became too much. Emma loved having her Grams around, but missed her old Mommy, the one who used to smile and laugh.

Six months after Mommy shot Daisy the hound dog to death on the living room floor, and three more dogs later, Daniel ran away. The authorities brought him back, but Social Services launched an investigation. Despite Daniel's outrageous claims about what went on in the house, the officials found nothing and closed the case. When Gram suggested they move to a different town, Mommy refused. She said she was tired of running. They would have to deal with the shadow people *here*. There was nowhere else to run.

A few weeks later, Emma tried to kill herself, swallowing a handful of pills she found in Grams' room. The old woman cried and wrung her hands, but Mommy took action, bending her youngest daughter over the tub and forcing her to vomit. The paramedics took her to the hospital and pumped her stomach, but they wouldn't let her leave. They admitted Emma to the mental hospital two towns away for a thirty day observation. It was a scary time for a little girl just shy of her eleventh birthday. She was the youngest patient in her ward. Mommy visited every day.

When she was still in the hospital, Emma heard the tell-tale sounds of the *bad ones* coming. She told Mommy, but there was nothing anyone could do. The *bad ones* entered an orderly that night, and the orderly killed two patients before security could stop him. He left Emma alone. Mommy wondered if Emma was too important for them to allow her to be killed. When the doctors released Emma three days later, all the nurses felt relieved. Though none of them could have articulated why, they were happy to see the quiet little girl go.

Grams baked a cake for Emma when she got home. It was chocolate, Emma's favorite. Everyone pretended to be happy for a while, even Mommy, her false smile bright but cheerless. Dark circles beneath their eyes had become a family characteristic, because no one slept much anymore. Mommy was skinnier even than she had been in high school, and Grams' face looked more lined every day. Dogs came and went. People died, but not anyone too close to the family. Things seemed to be calming down. They all settled into a familiar routine, and tried to live as normally as they could, at the same time dreading the next time the shadow people would visit.

Everyone looked forward to the time when Emma might no longer appeal to the poltergeists or demons or *whatever* they were. For a long while, the *bad ones* stopped coming. Even the *good ones* didn't seem to visit as often as they used to, and their antics became trivial and weak. Mommy rarely had to buy new dishes anymore.

As Emma's twelfth birthday passed, and then her thirteenth, the family began to repair their lives.

Emma sat at the table, absently pushing her food around the plate, as the rest of the family chatted about their day. She was trying to ignore their whispers she heard, hoping she was wrong. It had been such a long time since she'd heard them. An inky shadow oozed by, visible only in her peripheral vision, and she gasped, dropping her fork to the plate with a clatter. Her hands flew to her mouth in dismay.

Mommy and Grams stopped mid-conversation to look at her, taking in her round, fearful eyes with mounting alarm.

"What's up, Em? You okay?" Mommy stared at Emma, her face pinched in concern. Although Mommy had regained some of her former self over these quiet years, there were still lines of grief around her mouth and eyes that it seemed no amount of happiness could erase.

"Emma?" A seed of panic glimmered deep in Grams' eyes.

Unable to answer, Emma covered her face with her hands and burst into tears. It was Daniel who caught on first, his handsome face twisting in a fear-fueled rage.

"No! Not again!" his hands balled into fists at his sides. "IT'S SUPPOSED TO BE *OVER!*"

Mommy sat up straight, her eyes intense as they bored into her daughter, while Grams, dismayed, slumped back in her seat like a deflated balloon. All eyes were on Emma. The silence in the dining room became claustrophobic.

"Is it true? Are they back?" Mommy asked without inflection.

Emma nodded, not moving her hands from where they hid her face, silent sobs rocking her slender frame. Daniel stood abruptly and began to pace, his hands balling and flexing alternately. Grams joined Emma in her weeping.

"Who is it?" Mommy still leaned forward, but Emma shook her head, refusing to answer the question.

"I *need* to know, Emma. Tell me now."

When Emma looked up at her with those tear-filled eyes, and a heart-wrenching expression of horror, Mommy knew. There was no need to hear the words. Her mind whirled and she felt nauseous. Feelings of terror, agony, and acceptance all registered on her face within the space of a few seconds.

Grams began to shriek, her composure at an end. "Tell me! Who are they coming after? *Tell me!*"

Mommy said nothing, pushing back from the table and walking slowly across the room to retrieve the pistol from the drawer where she still kept it. *Just in case.* She laid it on the table in front of Grams before returning to the table and picking up her fork to eat again.

"Eat your dinner," Mommy said softly.

Grams became hysterical, looking at the gun as if she had never seen one before.

"Goddammit!" Grams yelled. "If someone doesn't talk to me I'm gonna scream!" She then stood her eyes bugging out in terror as she shrieked at them all. "Tell me who it is!"

Mommy looked up at Emma with haunted eyes, resignation marking her lined face.

The girl's tears flowed freely. She sucked in a sob to respond—

"*Mommy.*"

PUBLISHING HISTORY

"Chums", *Necrotic Tissue, Issue #11,* and in *The Best of Necrotic Tissue,* Stygian Publications, 2011.
"The Chopping Block", *For When the Veil Drops*, West Pigeon Press, 2012.
"Savior, Teach Us So to Rise", *Necrotic Tissue Issue #7*, Stygian Publications, 2009.
"Fireboomers", *Fifty-Two Stitches, Vol. 2,* Strange Publications, 2010.
"Pavement Ends" is new and exclusive to this collection.

"A Misadventure to Call Your Own", *Blood Lite III: Aftertaste,* ed. Kevin J. Anderson, Pocket Books, 2012
"Ghost Soup", *Gunslingers & Ghost Stories*, Science Fiction Trails, 2012
"You Don't Know Jack", *Crossed Genres*, 2009.
"There's No Word for It", *Bedtime Stories for Carrion Beetles*, CreateSpace, 2012.
"The Excitement Never Ends" is new and exclusive to this collection.

"A Wise Woman's Revenge", *SNM Horror Mag*, May 2011, and in *Wake the Witch*, May December Publications, 2012.
"Mommy", *Dark Moon Digest Presents GHOSTS,* Dark Moon Books, 2011.
"Sirens", *Dark Moon Digest*, Issue 4, July 2011.
"Mim's Room", *Best of Dark Moon Digest*, Dark Moon Books, 2012.
"To Each His Own Hell" is new and exclusive to this collection.

# ABOUT THE AUTHORS

ADRIAN LUDENS is a short story author and radio station program director & announcer. His collection, *Bedtime Stories for Carrion Beetles*, is available in multiple formats from Amazon and Smashwords. Recent anthology appearances include: *Shadows Over Main Street*, *Darker Edge of Desire*, *Surreal Worlds,* and *In Shambles*. A lifelong South Dakotan, he lives in Rapid City with his family. He enjoys horror, hockey, and heavy metal. Visit him at: *adrianludens.com*

A native of Rapid City, C.W. LASART now resides in Watertown, SD with her family and a menagerie of rescue pets. A lifelong fan of all things horror, her stories have been published by Cemetery Dance Publications, Dark Moon Digest, Eirelander Press and many others. She is a member of the Horror Writer's Association and also a member of the Bram Stoker Awards® Committee. For more information on her writing, go to *CWLasart.com* or drop her a line at **C.W.LaSart@hotmail.com**

DOUG MURANO, who was born and raised in South Dakota, makes his home in Rapid City. Since 2008, his stories have appeared in a number of venues, including *A Quick Bite of Flesh*, *Vignettes from the End of the World*, and *For When the Veil Drops*. Most recently, he co-edited an anthology of small-town Lovecraftian terror called *Shadows Over Main Street*, featuring multiple Bram Stoker Award®-winning authors, along with a number of new voices in horror. He is a member of the Horror Writers Association, is the organization's promotions and social media coordinator and the social media chair for the 2015 World Horror Convention/Bram Stoker Awards Weekend. Follow him on Twitter @muranofiction.

32379353R00135

Made in the USA
San Bernardino, CA
04 April 2016